Unbound

The Havoc Chronicles Book 2

Brant Williams

DEDICATION

For my mother,
who was always there when I needed her and loves me unconditionally.

CONTENTS

CHAPTER 1

OUT ON THE TOWN

I awoke in a bed that wasn't mine, rays of sunlight filtering through large windows framed by thin, lacy curtains. For a moment I simply lay there, not sure where I was, or how I had gotten there.

Then I heard shouting and the previous night's events came flooding back: The endless torrent of Bringers. Osadyn and Aata. Kara releasing the snare. Although I didn't recognize the room, I figured I was in one of the many bedrooms in the Berserker house.

With more effort than should have been necessary, I swung my legs over the edge of the bed and onto the floor.

The world spun, a dull ache pulsing at the back of my head. Nausea rose in my stomach, so I put my head in my hands, concentrating very hard on not projectile vomiting all over.

After a moment the worst of it appeared to be over, and I felt strong enough to stand. As I got up, I realized I was wearing a long nightgown that was definitely not mine. I had no recollection of how I got into it, but I sure hoped it was Mallika or Kara who put it on me.

I followed the sounds of arguing downstairs and into the large living room with the massive stone fireplace and overstuffed leather furniture.

Aata and Kara were locked in a massive shouting match, and from their appearance had only recently gotten out of bed themselves.

I took a step back, not wanting to intrude on their conversation, but there wasn't a place I could go in the house where I wouldn't overhear them screaming at each other. Unsure of what to do I simply stood there, out of sight, just around the corner.

"I was trying to save your life!" Kara shouted.

From my brief glance into the room, Aata had looked positively furious. I wouldn't have been surprised if any second he 'zerked.

"You had no right!" he shouted back.

Back and forth they yelled, Aata furious that Kara had released the snare and freed Osadyn, and Kara upset that Aata was angry at her for loving him enough to save him.

"It wasn't your choice to make!" Aata said. "I put my life on the line when I joined the Berserkers. We all did when we took the oaths. Some things are worth dying for."

"I couldn't just let you die," said Kara. "I love you!"

A crash and the sound of splintering wood reverberated through the house. "And that's why Berserkers and Binders should not get involved with each other!" shouted Aata. "I told you from the beginning that this would lead to trouble. Now you've ruined our one chance to capture Osadyn. All his future deaths are on your head!"

Heavy stomping footsteps crossed the floor. The front door was yanked open and slammed shut, shaking the house.

With Aata gone, the decibel level dramatically dropped. But the sound of Kara's muffled sobs pierced the silence, bringing tears to my own eyes.

I rushed into the living room and found her collapsed on the couch, sobbing uncontrollably. I sat down next to her and pulled her head onto my shoulder. I didn't say anything; I just held her and stroked her hair, brushing the stray strands out of her face.

Eventually Kara's sobs began to subside. She looked at me with tear-filled eyes and a sense of hopelessness. "He... he hates me, Madison," said Kara, and the sobs began again.

There was nothing for me to say, so I simply continued stroking her hair and making gentle hushing noises. Looking around the room, I saw a splintered hole in the floor and a broken chair. The frame had been split, the leather torn, and the stuffing was half out. I guessed it hadn't been Kara who had done that.

To be honest, I wasn't too happy with what Kara had done myself. I understood it – what if it had been someone I loved there – and in her position I probably would have done the same thing. But this morning, in the harsh light of day, just the thought of Osadyn getting away made me feel queasy about Kara's choice. Who knew how many people were going to die because we hadn't stopped him when we had the chance?

I was rescued from my comforting duties by Rhys, Shing, Mallika, and Eric arriving home with food for breakfast.

When Mallika saw us on the floor, her face changed from its normal stoic expression to one of pity. She reached down and pulled Kara to her feet. She and Eric guided Kara up the stairs to her bedroom, the crying growing fainter as they closed the door behind her.

The rest of the day was rather subdued. Aata didn't return and no one knew where he might have gone off to. Dad showed up around lunch time and gave me a big hug. He tried to cheer me up by telling me how brave I had been, but all I wanted to do was forget that last night had ever happened.

Once I had gone back home, I tried to call Amy and repair the damage I had done to our relationship by not being there when she desperately needed me. Unfortunately, she had already left to visit her Grandparents' farm in a tiny town in Kansas that we knew from past experience did not have cell phone reception. There was no way to contact her and make it right so it would have to wait until I saw her again at school.

If we needed proof that Osadyn was gone, the weather was all the evidence we needed. The temperature dropped down to a much more normal fifty degrees. Then, as if making up for being so warm, on New Year's Day, we got a couple of inches of rare snow that managed to last the entire afternoon before melting.

In addition to the temperature drop, the local news – which for the past few months had been full of assaults and murders – now seemed to be nothing but a non-stop holiday love-fest. Unlike the snow, that was a welcome change.

With Osadyn gone, there wasn't much reason for everyone to stay put. Yes it was possible – even probable – he would come back and attack, but the Berserker council wanted at least some of the Berserkers to once again go on the hunt for him.

There were many days of arguing and debate while the Berserkers tried to decide who should go and who should stay. They finally decided that Shing, Aata, and Eric would leave to actively search out Osadyn. There wasn't much they could do without Rhys' blood and Mallika's binding power, but it was to be purely a reconnaissance trip for the time being. Kara would stay because it was best for Kara and Aata to be apart for a while, and Rhys and Mallika would stay here because Osadyn might begin targeting me again.

With the logistics decided, Shing, Aata, and Eric left just before school started again, leaving the Berserker house feeling much emptier than before. While I was sad to see them leave, in some ways it was a relief. Aata's departure removed a source of tension and meant that Kara would now leave her room.

And, if I was honest with myself, I was eager to spend more time alone with Rhys now that Eric could not monopolize my attention.

The first day at school, I immediately sought out Amy to beg her forgiveness. I found her at her locker, her usual vivacious smile gone, replaced by a night-of-the-living-dead zombie-ish blank expression.

"Amy, I'm so sorry!" I blurted before she even had time to speak. "We were driving out of town when you called and we just left cell phone range. I tried to call when I got back but you were already in Kansas, and I couldn't get a hold of you. But I did leave several messages."

Knowing Amy for as long as I have, I knew she couldn't hold a grudge for very long, but I thought for sure she would pout and make me do a bit of pleading for forgiveness before thawing out. To my surprise, she gave me a smile and a big hug.

"I know," she said, and squeezed me tight.

"You do?" I pulled back to get a better look at her. This wasn't like Amy. Something was going on here.

"Yeah," she said. "The night I called, Rhys came by a couple of hours later to tell me he had dropped you off at an Aunt's house, and he told me how upset you were that we hadn't been able to talk. He stayed and listened to me babble on about what a jerk Cory was for almost an hour." She gave a sigh and leaned back against her locker. "It's too bad the boy is so clearly smitten with you, or else I would go after him myself."

Rhys had gone to see Amy while I was in the forest? Why hadn't he told me? It would have saved me a lot of worry if I had known.

Amy must have seen some of the concern on my face. "Oh, don't worry about him, that boy is crazy about you. I mean what kind of uber-perfect boyfriend would think to do something that sweet?" Her eyes tightened. "Not Cory, that's for sure."

Boyfriend? The word bounced around my head like a hummingbird with ADD, never staying still long enough for me to analyze it. Did he really tell Amy he was my boyfriend or was that

Amy making one of her usual – shockingly accurate – assumptions?

While Amy turned back to her locker and continued getting her books, I took in a few deep breaths. The last thing I needed now was to trigger a 'zerk in the middle of school. "Did, he, uh actually say that word?" I asked.

"What word?" Amy asked, not looking up from her preparations.

"Boyfriend." It came out rather higher-pitched squeakier than I had intended. I knew the minute the word came out of my mouth that I had said too much.

Amy looked up, a wicked gleam in her eye. I had her attention now. She paused and appeared to give the matter some thought. "I'm pretty sure," she said. "Does it really matter? I mean the boy has love-sick puppy written all over him." She gave me her most devious smile. "Unless you don't want him, of course?"

"No! I, uh..." I was too flustered to find words. Of course I wanted him. Who in their right mind wouldn't want someone like Rhys? But I still had those nagging feelings of self-doubt. I knew how I felt, but we had never actually talked about a relationship before. For all I knew any relationship we had could all be in my imagination. I didn't want to presume.

"Yes," said Amy, this time with a genuine smile.

"Yes, what?"

"He said the word 'boyfriend.'"

A warm giddy feeling washed over me. Our special moments weren't all in my imagination! He did care about me. That wonderful, almost magical, connection wasn't just some pent up schoolgirl fantasy playing out in my head – at least not entirely.

"Yeah, yeah," said Amy, closing her locker. "But keep in mind since you and Rhys are an item, that means Eric is now up for grabs, and I'm ready for a serious rebound."

We took a few steps down the hall before I answered her. "That might be difficult to do, unless you're looking for a long distance relationship."

Amy stopped and crossed her arms. "What do you mean?" she asked. "Spill."

When it had been decided that Eric would join the hunt for Osadyn, we knew we would have to come up with a good story to explain his disappearance. Eric wanted us to tell people he had been sacrificed by a ritualistic cult, but as usual we all ignored his suggestion.

"Eric is going to a military academy in Virginia for this semester," I said.

Amy gaped at me. "Military academy? Like the kind of places where they shave your head and make you run ten miles with a heavy pack in the middle of the night?"

I shrugged. "Something like that," I said. "I don't know all the details – it was rather sudden. Rhys told me he kept breaking house rules and something bad happened on Christmas Eve so they sent him there to learn some discipline."

Once the initial excitement of new gossip was over, Amy seemed to deflate. "Well, so much for rebound option number one," she said. Suddenly she brightened. "Hey, why don't we forget about boys for a while and do something together, just the two of us?" she suggested. "Like old times."

"You really want to go back to old times?" I asked. "You and me as spokespeople for the hopelessly undateable? I'll pass, thanks."

"Not that," she said. "You and me go and have a girls' night out. No boys allowed."

"Sure, why not?" I said, with what I hoped was an enthusiastic voice. Actually I could think of several really good reasons why not, the foremost of those being my desire to spend time with Rhys, but Amy was my best friend. She was trying to be tough, but I could tell she still needed me.

"This will be fun!" Amy put an arm around my shoulder. "Look out world, Madison and Amy are going out on the town."

Over the next few days we solidified our plans. I was hoping for a laid back evening spent watching romantic movies and crying our eyes out, but Amy wanted to "get out and do something." We settled on dinner and shopping in Portland Friday night.

Getting permission to do that was not so easy. Dad and Rhys were both against it, but that made me all the more determined to make it happen. I had spent the last several months under constant surveillance. Osadyn was gone – it was time for my parole to begin.

"Can Rhys at least come with you?" Dad asked. As much as I liked the idea, I knew Amy wouldn't want it, so I shot that idea down in a hurry.

"This is a girls' night, Dad," I said. "Not only would Rhys hate it, but the entire point of this trip is to do something fun without any boys around."

I was glad I had started early, because it took most of the week to wear them both down. But my logic was sound: Osadyn was clearly gone – significantly colder temperatures as proof – and I was a Berserker, which meant it was safer for me to wander around downtown Portland than it was for Dad.

By Friday night they had given in – if not willingly – to my demands, and Amy and I drove my mom's car down to the Pearl District – a sort of urban-chic hipster neighborhood with plenty of art galleries, shopping, and restaurants.

Amy wanted Thai food so we went to a little place off of Hoyt street that had recently opened up. Amy was more adventurous and tried one of the spicy dishes, but I stuck with my usual Pad Thai. I hadn't eaten Thai since I had become a Berserker and I hoped it wouldn't be too strong for my enhanced sense of taste.

Despite the fact that Amy had wanted this to be a girls' night out with no boys, she sure had a hard time not talking about them. She told me all about Cory and how he had gradually gotten meaner during the semester until that last night when he had shoved her down.

"And now he has the nerve to call up begging for forgiveness," she said, and thrust her fork into a piece of chicken as if it had personally offended her.

I tried to persuade her to give him a second chance, especially since I knew it was partially my fault he'd been acting that way. But without revealing the key fact that her boyfriend had been influenced by the prolonged presence of a monstrous demon, I didn't really have much of a case.

After dinner we walked through the streets looking in shop windows and occasionally going inside for a closer look. In the end we didn't buy anything because the prices for everything were unbelievable. We were used to shopping at the mall and everything here was quite a bit more expensive.

I remembered Eric's revelation that as a Berserker I'd inherited some sort of trust fund, but I hadn't heard any mention of it since, and Dad certainly hadn't brought it up. So, in the meantime I was going to have to continue in my teenage poverty.

After a while Amy got discouraged by the prices. She had never had much money and was hoping to find a good bargain for the last of the income from her summer job. To take her mind off of clothing, I suggested we stop at Powell's Bookstore. To my surprise, Amy agreed.

We hopped on the MAX, Portland's light rail, and rode over to Powell's, one of my favorite places in the world. To call it simply a bookstore didn't do it justice. They called it the City of Books, and that wasn't much of an exaggeration. It took up an entire city block and extended several stories upwards. It was my own personal haven. I could spend hours there and never get bored.

Together we wandered through the rooms browsing through thousands of titles packed onto row after row of shelves.

By the time we'd finished, it was getting late and we decided to head home. A thick fog had rolled in while we were inside, turning the night eerie and damp. The night air surrounded us and coated us with moisture as we walked back to the MAX stop.

With the fog as thick as it was, we accidentally missed our stop and had to get off one stop farther than we'd intended. It was only a few blocks so we decided to walk rather than wait for a train back.

"Thanks for tonight," said Amy as we walked. "I know you have better things to do than hang with me, but it felt good to be back together again. No boys getting in the way of our sisterhood."

Before I could reply, a large man stepped out of a nearby alley holding a knife in his hand. He wore jeans and a black hooded sweatshirt pulled over his head, obscuring his face.

"What are two attractive young ladies doing out here all alone at night?" he asked, casually holding his knife as if he were simply going to use it to clean his nails. His voice sounded merely curious, but it was glaringly obvious he was trying to intimidate us with his presence and physical size.

Amy hesitated, but I grabbed her arm and began to steer her around the man. The sound of a click from behind brought us up short.

"The man asked you a question," said a raspy voice from behind. Amy let out a soft gasp as a second man stuck the barrel of a gun in my back. She looked up at me, her eyes bulging and terrified. As girls living outside of the city, this was the kind of situation we had been warned about our entire lives but never actually expected to encounter.

I tried to turn around, but the man grabbed me by the back of the neck and steered me towards the alley. After the first moment of initial shock I became more annoyed than anything. I was a trained Berserker. I had fought Osadyn and hundreds of Bringers and come out with hardly a scratch – I didn't count the fact that I had practically passed out from exhaustion afterwards. I could take out both of these creeps with nothing more than my thumb.

The only thing that prevented me from 'zerking right then and there was Amy. As a Berserker I was bullet proof – at least in theory, I hadn't ever tested it out – but Amy wasn't quite as durable. If I 'zerked, the guy with the knife might hurt Amy out of panic. Also, I might have a hard time explaining to her the whole glowing freak thing.

Behind me I heard Amy's muffled squeal as the man with the knife dragged her along into the alley with us. The man with the gun shoved me up against a wall, and the man with the knife did the same to Amy.

The man with a gun held me and Amy at gunpoint, while the man with the knife retrieved a paper bag and pulled out a roll of duct tape. He placed it over our mouths and bound our hands behind our backs.

While this was happening, I took a closer look at the man with the gun. He seemed to be in his thirties with long brown hair and a scar on his neck almost like a gruesome necklace. He wore jeans with a dark sweater.

But the thing that struck me the most was his eyes. Cold and hard, they showed neither mercy nor pity. His mouth was turned up into a smile – the sick creep was enjoying this.

He noticed me watching and leered at me, licking his lips in hopes of frightening me. And if I were a normal girl it almost certainly would have worked. But I was anything but normal. I gave him my best flat stare to show him that I would not be intimidated.

"Oh, you are a feisty one," he said walking closer to me. "This is going to be fun."

While he was distracted with me, Amy had been scooting closer to the mouth of the alley. Her mouth was taped and her hands were bound, but her legs were still free. When the man with the gun moved towards me, she took the opportunity to run.

The man with the knife swore and ran after her, catching her before she could get to the end of the alley. He hit her on the back of the head with the handle of his knife and she dropped to the ground in a heap.

Only the tape prevented me from screaming. Seeing Amy collapse to the ground I felt hot anger rush through me. My kind, innocent Amy had been assaulted and who knew what kind of damage it had caused?

The 'zerk came easily, and I embraced the power. The alley lit up with my glow, and I ripped through the duct tape like tissue paper.

Both men goggled at me, taking several steps back. The one with the gun raised it and shot me.

The bullet hit me in the shoulder, but I hardly felt the impact. It punched a hole in my blouse, but then crumpled against my skin and fell to ground with a ping.

Both men turned around and ran for the alley exit, but they might as well have been moving in slow motion. With ease I raced ahead of them and cut them off from leaving the alley. They scrambled to stop before reaching me, then turned around and ran back the other way, hoping to escape out the back. I picked up a massive dumpster and tossed it past them so that it landed with a metallic crash in their path, spewing garbage everywhere. Frantically, they began climbing the dumpster and were almost over the top by the time I got there.

I grabbed them by the backs of their clothing and lifted them up in the air, one in each hand. For a moment I was so angry that I was tempted to smash them into the walls. Wasn't death an appropriate punishment for scum like this? Who knew how many other girls they had attacked?

I turned them towards me and looked up into their faces. The malice and confidence were gone, replaced by simple abject terror. Terror of me – of what I might do to them.

"Please don't kill me," said the man who had had the knife. He didn't have it any longer. Tears ran down his face, and he was practically blubbering. The other man was looking to the sky and muttering what sounded like a prayer under his breath.

From behind me I heard a moan, and looked back to see Amy beginning to move. Knowing that she was alive and about to regain consciousness, I moved quickly. I slammed the two men together – not nearly as hard as I wanted to – and then dropped them to the ground. I didn't know if they were unconscious or simply playing dead, and to be honest I didn't really care.

I reached up and pulled down the fire escape. Not the ladder – the entire fire escape. It ripped from the building in mostly one piece, breaking where it had been bolted in. Working as fast as only a Berserker could, I twisted the metal pieces together to create a cage and placed it on top of the two men. I placed the dumpster on top of the cage to be sure they couldn't lift it up. I took one of the leftover metal bars and scratched the word "rapists" into the cement in front of my makeshift cage. Let's see what the police made of that when they were found.

I ripped off the tape, and scooped Amy's limp body in my arms, ready to run from there as quickly as I could. I needed to get Amy to a hospital and have her checked out. But before I had taken more than a few steps, I felt a nearby Berserker moving towards me.

Up ahead I saw a bright glow hurtling through the fog. I recognized the figure at once – who else could it have been? Rhys stopped in front of me, his varé drawn and at the ready, his eyes trying to look everywhere at once. With the glow surrounding him, he was breathtaking. A vision of male perfection – deadly, beautiful, and – what was he doing here?

"Were you following me?" I demanded. It was the only way he could have arrived so quickly. Berserkers were fast, but he wouldn't be here yet unless he had been lurking nearby.

In an instant, Rhys switched from alpha predator searching for quarry, to hunted prey on the defensive. His eyes met mine, and an expression of embarrassed discomfort crossed his face. He looked like the proverbial little boy caught with his hand in the cookie jar.

"Not exactly," he said, but the tone of his voice made it clear that I had it exactly right.

"Did my dad put you up to this?"

Rhys took a step back and raised his hands in a gesture of surrender. A gesture that looked especially strange when done by a glowing Berserker carrying a weapon. "No," he said. "It was nothing like that. I came down here on my own."

"So, you didn't think I could take care of myself?" Given what had just happened, this was kind of an unfair accusation, but the truth was that I was not too happy at the moment.

Amy stirred in my arms, turning my attention back to the situation at hand.

"We'll talk about this later," I said, and then filled him in on what had happened.

As I spoke, Rhys' eyes narrowed and his jaw clenched. He understood what those two had been planning as well as I did.

"How badly is Amy hurt?" he asked.

"I don't know," I said. "I was going to take her to a hospital and get some help."

Rhys took in a deep breath. I could tell he was thinking the same thing I was – that taking Amy into the hospital would bring up a whole lot of awkward questions. "Amy's health is the number one priority right now," he said. "Get her to a hospital as quickly as you can." He looked past me into the alley where the two men were caged. "I need a moment to visit these two gentlemen."

I didn't know what Rhys intended to do, but from the look of calculated determination on his face, it wouldn't be pleasant.

I had no problem with that.

As I ran I tried to avoid populated areas, but I only had a vague idea of the general direction I needed to go, and so I accidentally passed a few startled pedestrians. I simply kept going since there was nothing I could do about it right now.

But before I could find a hospital, Amy's movements became stronger and she started to wake up. I changed from a full 'zerk to the less powerful, but more importantly, less glowy pre-zerk.

Amy immediately started thrashing. "Let me go!" she yelled. "Get off me!"

I slowed to a stop. "Hey, Amy, it's me," I said. "You're safe." I gently set her down on her feet, making sure she was completely steady before I let go. She frantically looked around in every direction before finally taking a deep shuddering breath and bursting into tears.

"Shhhh," I said, pulling her into a hug in an attempt to comfort her and calm her down. "We're fine. They aren't coming after us."

For several minutes Amy continued to sob into my shoulder until she had finally cried herself out and pulled back wiping her eyes with the back of her hand.

"Why are we not dead?" she asked. "How did we get away?" She reached up and winced as she rubbed the back of her head where the man had hit her.

I really wanted to tell her the truth, but I knew that wouldn't go over very well with Dad and the Berserkers. I would have to go with a combination of vagueness and complete lies.

"You started to sneak away and the guy with the knife hit you on the head," I said.

"Yeah, I remember that far," said Amy. "Next thing I knew you were carrying me. It's the in between that's blank."

It was time for some quick thinking. I took a deep breath. "I screamed after you were hit, and then I heard someone yelling asking what was wrong. I heard footsteps running towards us and the two men got scared and ran out of the alley. I wasn't going to wait for them to come back, so I picked you up and ran in the opposite direction. That's when you woke up." During my explanation, Amy had stared at the ground in an unfocused way that made me nervous. She had been hit in the head and who knew what kind of damage that had done. I lifted her chin and looked into her eyes. "I think we need to get you to a hospital and get your head checked out."

Amy shook her head. "No, I'm fine. Look, I don't have any slurred speech, headache, vomiting, or spontaneous combustion." She smiled at me. "I don't have a concussion, but if it will make you feel better, I promise I'll let my mom look at me when we get home."

I hesitated. Amy's Mom was a nurse and Amy often spouted off obscure medical facts she had learned. Now that she had snapped out of the initial shock she seemed to be fine, but what did I know? It's not like I was a medical professional.

"You promise you'll let her look you over?" I asked.

"Promise," she said, her face a mask of seriousness. She held up her hand in the Boy Scout sign. "Scout's honor."

Amy could only keep a straight face for so long, and she burst out laughing. It wasn't her usual laugh and there was a bit of a hysterical edge to it that worried me, but after a moment I couldn't help it and joined in. Together we laughed long and hard, tears streaming down our faces. The joke wasn't very funny, but the laughter felt wonderful – some of the tension of the night easing out of us.

Eventually our laughter subsided, occasionally erupting in a short burst of giggles. I could tell now that Amy would be okay, and I was grateful for that – it had been a close call. But as we walked back to the car, I had the strong feeling – or maybe it was more of an impression – that the consequences of what had happened tonight were not over. I shuddered as the feeling came over me, desperately hoping it was just my over-active imagination.

I could not have been more wrong.

CHAPTER 2

HAZE

I awoke the next day with a sick knot of apprehension in my stomach. When I had arrived home last night I told Dad what had happened and he had reacted with typical parental horror, telling me that I was never allowed to go downtown by myself again. That lasted until I 'zerked and lifted his chair, with him still in it, above my head.

He got the point.

Still, the fact was that I – in all my glowing splendor – had been seen by several unknown pedestrians and had ripped down an entire fire escape last night. Something was likely to end up on the news. Not an ideal situation.

Sure enough, when I went down for breakfast my dad had the TV on to the local news and the DVR paused on the story of two men found in a cage.

The reporter explained that a passerby found them around 5:00 am and alerted the police. The men were actually still in the cage. The rescue team was awaiting a portable crane to lift the dumpster off because they feared cutting the bars might cause the structure to collapse, crushing the men beneath.

"But the really strange part about all this," said the reporter. "Is that these men claim to have been trapped here by a glowing girl with some sort of super powers."

The camera switched to the cage, which was surrounded by policemen, paramedics, and firefighters. All I could really see was the dumpster on top of the cage.

"The officer who first arrived on the scene also saw this." They flashed a picture of the word "Rapists" I had scratched into the cement. "While neither man would provide ID to the police, we are now hearing reports that both of them are confessing to several assaults and are actually *asking* to be locked up."

Dad turned off the TV and turned to face me. "You do realize what a mess this is, don't you?"

"I'm sorry, but when he hit Amy, I snapped." Well, I was kind of sorry. I was sorry it was getting so much publicity, but I was not sorry for what I put those scum through. Looking back I actually wished I had done more, or at least been a bit more creative about terrorizing them.

I wondered what Rhys had done to them to make them so eager to confess.

When Rhys stopped by for lessons later that day, the concern in his eyes was easy to read, but I wasn't letting him off that easily.

"So?" I said, once we were alone in the practice room. I folded my arms and waited for a reply.

Rhys met my gaze head-on without flinching. Finally after a moment, he looked away. "Okay," he said. "I was following you."

"Why?"

Rhys threw up his arms in exasperation. "Why? After what happened last night you are really asking me why?"

"I see, so you knew in advance that Amy and I were going to be assaulted? Do Berserkers have some sort of precognitive powers that I'm not aware of?"

"Look, it's not like that," said Rhys.

"Then tell me what it is like."

"Obviously I didn't think you and Amy would be attacked. But I was still worried for your safety."

"But why?" I asked. "What were you worried about?"

"Osadyn," said Rhys. "I know he's gone for now, but Shing, Aata, and Eric have had no success in tracking him down. That means he's on the move. Which means he could easily show up, capture you, and be gone before we even knew he was there." He looked at the ground. "It wouldn't be the first time it had happened like that."

"That still doesn't give you the right to follow me," I said. I knew he had only been trying to protect me, but I was furious he'd done it behind my back.

With a sigh, Rhys opened the little refrigerator we kept in the practice room and pulled out a bottle of water. "I kept as far away from you as I could," he said. "All I wanted to do was be close enough to feel you 'zerk if you were in danger. That's a pretty big range. I figured if I hung around in the same general area, it would be enough." He took a drink and set it down on a table. "I'm sorry, I shouldn't have followed you without your permission."

And with that, my annoyance drained away. Yeah, I didn't like what he had done, but I really liked the fact that he could admit when he was wrong. That was a trait that seemed to be in short supply in the male gender – or maybe it was something that just took a hundred years to develop.

I smiled. "Thanks. That means a lot to me."

Rhys nodded and looked relieved. "How are you?" he asked.

I shrugged. "Fine, I suppose. Dad's not too pleased about the news reports, but there's not much I can do about it right now."

"I'm not worried about your Dad's reaction," said Rhys. "How are you? I know you've got power and can't really be hurt by humans, but these kinds of experiences do more than just physical damage." He took my hands and looked deeply into my eyes. I knew he was waiting for an answer, but I couldn't concentrate on anything other than the feel of his hands on mine and the overwhelming wish that he would pull me in closer.

But our moment was just that – a moment. He gave my hands a last squeeze and let go, breaking our connection. I fixed the moment in my mind, memorizing all the details before they faded so that I could recall it later. Who knew when something like this might happen again?

"Are you sure you're okay, Madison?" he asked.

The truth was that I was more worried about Amy than myself. I was fine. I didn't have nightmares or difficulty sleeping. Amy, however, wasn't returning my calls. "Honestly, I'm fine," I said. "I'm more worried about Amy's reaction than mine. It was strange, the only fear I felt was that Amy might get hurt. I guess after fighting Osadyn and a rushing ocean of Bringers, fighting a couple of thugs seems a bit anti-climactic."

Rhys looked at me skeptically, clearly not believing that I could be that nonchalant about the situation. Given how protective he and my dad were, likely the only thing that would convince them that I was fine was time.

"One last question," I said. "What did you do to the guys after I left with Amy?"

Rhys' face split into a mischievous grin. It was a different look, but one that suited him. Who was I kidding? Everything looked good on Rhys.

"I just made sure they understood that if they weren't in jail by the end of the day that they would quickly discover there are worse things than a prison sentence. Much worse."

He shrugged and flicked his varé open. "Ready to train?"

I was tempted to ask for details, but I figured I could fill in the blanks well enough. Besides, I was enjoying looking at that smile. I opened my varé and stood in a defensive stance. "Let's do it."

***

Amy called me on Sunday, having just seen the news.

"Do you think it's them?" she asked. "The ones who attacked us?"

I had to handle this carefully. I wasn't worried that Amy would figure out I was a Berserker – the possibility of real-life superpowers would never cross her mind – but I didn't want her to know that the men who had attacked us really were the ones in the cage. It would bring up too many awkward questions.

"I don't think so," I said. "I got a good look at the guy with the gun, and he had a dark beard." I sure hoped she didn't get a good look and call my bluff. "The guys on TV didn't have beards, and I doubt they had any way of shaving in that cage."

"I guess so," said Amy. "Are you sure it wasn't the same person? It was kind of dark and hard to see, and it seems an awfully big coincidence for there to be more attackers in that same area on the same night."

"I'm positive," I said. "You're right. It was dark and hard to see. But after you were knocked out, our guys heard someone coming, and they started running. The gunman's hood fell down and I got a good look at his face. It wasn't either of those guys."

That seemed to satisfy Amy, or at least it stopped her from asking me more questions. I hoped she would let it go. Otherwise, I would have to ask Kara or Mallika to cast a haze on her.

***

I had hoped that the story would die down before school on

Monday, but developments over the weekend kept it fresh in the news. The men were convicted sex offenders from California who had violated parole by traveling to Portland. Their pleas to be locked up, and their claims that a glowing girl attacked them made for sensational headlines. The story not only hit the local news, but also got a few mentions at the national level.

When Rhys picked me up for school, I was grateful that he didn't ask any more questions about my emotional state. Between my concerns about Amy and the stress of the constant news coverage, the attack on Friday night was the last thing I wanted to discuss.

Apparently not too many of the kids at school paid attention to the news, because I didn't hear anyone discussing it in the halls as I walked in.

All thoughts of Friday night were pushed to the back of my mind as Rhys and I walked to Physics that morning. We had just passed the drinking fountains when we met Josh walking down the hallway in the opposite direction.

Ever since he had started dating Ginger, by a sort of silent mutual agreement, Josh and I had stopped all communication. Whenever we crossed paths, we did our best to pretend we hadn't seen each other. What was left for us to say? You can only apologize so many time to a boy for smashing him into a tree.

Today, instead of looking away, Josh kept his eyes locked on me as we passed, even turning to look behind him as I walked by. It wasn't a friendly or flirting kind of look - those days were long gone. No, his expression was cold and blank, his emotions as inaccessible as a James Joyce novel.

"What was that all about?" asked Rhys.

"I have no idea," I said. I kept my eyes forward and continued walking, but I had a strong feeling that if I turned around, I would see Josh still standing there, a lonely island in a sea of moving people, his eyes never leaving me.

I didn't turn around.

At lunch that afternoon Josh's strange behavior made me even more uncomfortable. I sat in my usual spot and tried to have a normal conversation with Rhys. The operative word here was *tried*. I couldn't help noticing that Josh was looking over at me far more often than normal. I tried to ignore him, but my distraction must have been pretty obvious because Rhys finally turned around to see what I kept looking at.

He turned back to me with a rather amused look on his face. "Ahh, Josh. Now I see why you've been so distracted during lunch." He looked down at the table, the smile slowly fading from his face. "Do you still have feelings for him?" he asked.

"Does nausea count?" I asked.

Rhys gave me a skeptical look. "Do you really expect me to believe that? I've seen the way you two so carefully pretend the other one isn't there when you think someone is watching. There are obviously still some unresolved feelings."

"There's nothing between us," I said. I frantically searched for a new topic. I wasn't terribly experienced in this area, but I was pretty sure most guys didn't want to hear about their girlfriends' ex-boyfriends – they tended to get territorial and find ridiculously stupid ways of marking their territory.

Not that we were even officially dating, but Amy had said that Rhys had claimed to be my boyfriend. Or was that just an excuse to explain why we spent so much time together?

Rhys gave a small shrug. "If you say so."

I opened my mouth to reply, but shut it again as Josh stood up from his table and walked over to us with the appearance of someone who was preparing for a heated battle to the death.

"Madison, can I talk to you for a minute," Josh said. He gave Rhys a distrustful look. "Alone?"

"Uh, sure," I said. Rhys leaned back in his chair and folded his arms, clearly unwilling to move. "Let's go out in the hall."

We wound our way through the maze of lunch tables and out of the cafeteria. It was quieter out in the hall and the temperature was several degrees cooler. We walked part way down the corridor before I spoke.

"What are you doing?" I asked. It came out sounding harsher than I had intended. "You know Ginger is going to throw a fit when she finds out that we've been talking. It may not mean that much to you, but she's pretty good at making my life miserable."

Josh put his hands on his hips and looked at me, no hint of a smile on his face. I cringed when I saw his expression. What had happened to that happy, good-natured guy that I had dated? He used to be so fun and now he seemed so serious all the time.

"This is more important than Ginger," he said. "Where were you

Friday night?"

Sudden comprehension dawned on me. The attack. He must have seen the news and made the obvious connection. "What are you talking about?" I said.

Although I didn't think it was possible, his face grew even sterner. "You know what I'm talking about, Madison. Friday night two men were attacked by a glowing girl with superhuman strength. I don't know about you, but I only know of one person who fits that description."

Well, so much for plausible denial. It was time to jump to the alibi. "All right, if you have to know I was out with Amy on Friday."

"I know it was you," said Josh. "Look, I've kept your secret because you promised me it would never get out of control. But you could have hurt those men."

Okay, this was too much. He was worried about me hurting them? The unjustness of it was too much.

"Look," I said, a note of anger creeping into my voice. "Those guys attacked us and dragged us into an alley at gun point to do who-knows-what. They were convicted sex-offenders! If I hadn't used my powers, you can bet there would be grief counselors here and you would have spent all day in an assembly mourning the deaths of two students."

Josh seemed taken aback. "That's not the point," he said.

"Oh, what is?"

"The point," he said, "is that your powers are out of control. You're a danger to yourself and those around you. I mean, you practically destroyed a building."

I could not believe we were having this conversation. I had defended myself and Amy from assault and he thought I was the out-of-control bad guy here?

"I did not destroy a building. I just pulled down the fire escape." Okay, when I put it that way it did sound bad. But I was clearly justified and never "out of control".

"I'm sorry, Madison, but I don't think I can let this go on anymore. I don't see this going anywhere good."

"You can't 'let this go on anymore'? What are you saying, Josh?"

"I'm saying that if you don't turn yourself in and get some help, I'm going to call the police and tell them what I know." He paused and ran both hands though his hair in frustration. It didn't help my mood that I noticed how cute he was when he did that.

All my frustration vanished. Instead of angry I felt sick, like I had been kicked in the stomach and was going to throw up. "You would really do that?"

He nodded. "It's for your own good, Madison. This has to stop before you or someone you care about gets hurt. Turn yourself in and get some help. It will be easier for everyone." And with that parting shot he turned around and started walking back into the cafeteria.

"Josh, wait," I said, reaching out a hand after him. I desperately needed him to stay. I couldn't let him leave like this. If only I could make him forget that night had ever happened.

Blue mist shot out of my palms forming a billowing cloud that swirled around Josh and then suddenly constricted, sinking into him.

Josh stopped walking and simply stood there, unmoving. What had I done? I ran after him and grabbed his shoulders, looking into his glassy eyes – eyes like I had seen on my mom the night Mallika had cast a haze on her.

I looked around the hall, hoping no one had seen what I had just done. Then I remembered that only a Binder could see the blue mist of the haze.

Now I just had to remember how to make the haze work. I had seen Mallika do this with my mom, and Kara had explained the basic theory to me, but I was still terrified that I would somehow mess it up and turn Josh into a mindless puppet.

I thought about asking Rhys for help, but I didn't dare leave Josh alone like this, and when I looked at the clock I saw that I only had a couple minutes before the bell rang and the hall became flooded with students. I had to do this now.

I took a deep breath and spoke. "Madison is a Berserker. She can glow and has super strength. When you two were dating, she started glowing and accidentally hurt you. After that you told her to go away. She left and you broke up with her and started dating Ginger." Oops. Should I have said anything about Ginger? Well, there was no turning back now. "Recently you saw on the news that some men were attacked by a glowing girl and you think it's Madison."

I paused, trying to remember if there was anything else I should say. There was less than a minute left before the bell rang – I needed to end this quickly. I lifted my hands and clapped them together in front of Josh's face, the way Mallika had done with my mom. That had seemed to be some sort of ending signal. Josh blinked in surprise and without a word turned and walked down the hallway.

"What was that all about?" asked Rhys when I went back to our table. The bell rang so there was no time to explain. "I'll tell you later," I said and grabbed my trash.

I didn't see Josh for the rest of the day, which was just as well, and when Rhys tried to bring up the subject, I managed to find excuses not to talk at the moment. I didn't like hiding this from Rhys, but I had promised Mallika that I wouldn't tell anyone about my Binder powers until we knew more.

By the time we got into the car I could tell Rhys wasn't going to let the subject drop. He had that stubborn look on his face that gave him a dark, brooding presence that I found extremely attractive. The down side was that I also knew that he meant business. He was going to find out what had happened, whether I wanted to tell him or not.

Sure enough, the moment we got into the car Rhys said, "So, what happened with Josh?"

I had expected this and so I had prepared a suitable story to explain what had happened. I had heard somewhere that the best lies were mostly truth, so I decided to go that route. It was time to put my acting skills to the test.

"Josh heard about the men who attacked me on the news." All completely true.

"And?"

"And he figured out that the girl who started glowing must have been me." Also true.

Rhys turned to face me in the car. His beautiful eyes fixed on mine, concern radiating from him. It was really too bad all this was happening. I would have much rather simply enjoyed looking at him.

"And what did he think about that?" asked Rhys. "Is he going to keep your secret?"

Here's where the lies came in. "Well, at first he wanted me to turn myself in. But once I explained that I had just been defending myself, he calmed down. He just wanted to make sure I wasn't turning into the Incredible Hulk or something."

Rhys visibly relaxed, a wry smile appearing. "Well, not only are you cuter than the Hulk, but I'm sure you could take him in a one-on-one grudge match."

I leaned against Rhys' shoulder and sighed dramatically. "You sure know how to make a girl feel special."

He put his arm around me, pulling me closer. It was hard to concentrate on the joke when all I really wanted to do was to sink into his arms and stay there for as long as humanly – or was that Berserkerly? – possible.

"Yeah," he said with heavy sarcasm in his voice, "you've seen how smooth I am with the ladies."

I pulled back a little so I could see his face. "Do you really not understand the effect you have on girls?"

"I think you've got me mistaken for Eric. He's the one all the girls swoon over."

I shook my head. Boys are dumb.

***

The next day started out wonderfully. The morning news didn't even mention the story about our attackers, which meant it had gone from news to history. I was perfectly fine with that because it meant that we had escaped with less exposure than we had feared. If it hadn't been for Josh, it would have been a clean getaway.

When Rhys and I arrived at school, we headed straight for my locker. I dropped off my coat and backpack and got out the books I needed for class. When I closed my locker and turned around, coming down the hallway was a sight I hadn't seen in months – Josh smiling. He looked like himself again, something I hadn't seen since the night I'd first injured him. The sullen, moody Josh of the past several months had vanished overnight.

Feeling extremely relieved that I seemed to have cast the haze correctly, I watched Josh's approach. He high-fived, fist bumped, and slapped people on the rear as he walked by. The reaction was incredible – a couple of sophomores actually started applauding as he walked by. Clearly I wasn't the only one who missed the old Josh.

I expected him to continue down the hall when he got to me, but to my surprise – and horror – he walked right up to me, an infectious grin lighting up his face.

"How's it going?" he asked.

I looked over at Rhys to see his reaction, but he didn't look hurt or angry – more curious and confused.

"I'm fine," I said. "You sure seem to be in a good mood."

"Well, now that you mention it, I am," he said. "Can I talk to you alone for a second?"

I looked around at the crowded hallway and shrugged. "I kind of doubt it. Besides, I don't think Ginger would like that too much."

Josh laughed. "I'm not too worried about her."

I glanced over at Rhys and he shrugged. He didn't seem to have any idea what this was about either. "I'll see you in class," he said and gave my hand a squeeze before walking away.

"So what's going on?" I asked.

Josh casually leaned against the lockers. "I've been thinking a lot since yesterday," he said.

Not exactly the words I wanted to hear. Clearly I had messed up casting the haze if he could remember it. My mind raced, searching desperately for a solution. I could try casting a haze again, but the hall was so crowded that it would be tough to do. Besides, if I didn't get it right the first time, what were the odds of doing it right in a noisy hallway crammed with students?

"Listen," I said, keeping my voice low. "I know you think my powers are out of control, but I promise you I'm not going to hurt anyone."

When I mentioned my powers, Josh's eyes glazed. When I finished speaking, he shook his head as if trying to clear his thoughts and continued on like I hadn't even said a word.

"Like I said, I've been thinking a lot about you since yesterday."

Now I was really confused. From his reaction, it sure seemed like the haze was working. But if he didn't know about my powers anymore, why would he want to talk to me?

"Anyway, I know we broke up, but I've been thinking about it, and I can't even remember the reason *why* we broke up." He took a deep breath and gave me a tentative smile. "So, I was hoping that maybe we could get back together and give it another try. What do you think?"

CHAPTER 3

ACTING OUT

A nd there they were, the words I had desperately wanted to hear for so long. Only now instead of bringing me blissful happiness, they felt more like a punch in the stomach.

"But Josh, what about Ginger?" How much of his memory had the haze affected?

He shrugged, seemingly unconcerned. "That's not a problem. I'll just break up with her." His brow furrowed in confusion. "To be honest, I really don't remember why I started dating her."

This was bad. The haze was supposed to make him forget about my powers, not fall in love with me! I really must have messed something up to get this kind of reaction.

"Uh, Josh, I don't think getting back together is such a great idea," I said.

"Why not? We were good together."

His blunt answer stopped me in my tracks. The truth was, we *had* been good together. For so many years he had been my fantasy crush, so far above me on the social ladder that I had no possibility of ever reaching him. For the briefest time we had been together, and I had been genuinely happy. Then my powers had shown up and ruined everything.

And there was my answer.

It was my powers that broke us up. Now that he had no memory of my powers, his mind had a hole in it that didn't understand what had happened. As far as he was concerned, we could continue our relationship right where we left off.

I blushed as I remembered that first kiss. It had been sweet and wonderful – until I 'zerked and almost killed him.

The warning bell rang, interrupting my thoughts.

"I, uh, I've got to get to class," I said and rushed down the hall towards the Physics classroom.

The bell rang right as I slid into my seat, so there was no opportunity to tell Rhys what had happened. Which, given my current state of emotional turmoil, was fine with me.

"That was cutting it close, Miss Montgomery," Mr. Shumway said.

I did my best to pay attention in class, but it was tough to keep my mind focused on angles of reflection and refraction when it kept drifting back to my conversation with Josh.

The worst part was that I felt really torn about the whole thing. Josh had been my first and longest crush. But things were finally starting to progress with Rhys – extremely slowly – but he had told

Amy that he was my boyfriend. That had to mean something.

When the bell rang, I hurried toward American History. Instead of going to his class, Rhys walked with me. Ordinarily this would make my heart skip a few beats, but I knew he wanted to find out what had happened with Josh, and I had no desire to talk about it yet.

"So, what did Josh want?" he asked.

Yep, exactly the one topic I didn't want to discuss. "Aren't you going to be late for class?" I asked, trying to change the subject.

"Probably, but seeing as how I don't actually need a high school diploma, my grades hardly matter. I'm here to protect you."

"Well, if you don't need a diploma, then clearly I don't either, right? I mean what use does a Berserker have for a high school education?" I just needed to stall a little bit longer, then I could avoid telling Rhys what happened until lunch. Of course I knew my procrastination was completely childish and would likely catch up and bite me hard in sensitive parts of my anatomy, but at the moment I didn't care.

Rhys looked pensive and then grabbed my arm and stopped in the middle of the hall. "You're right," he said. "This whole education thing is a bit of a joke. Let's get out of here and tell your dad you've decided to drop out." He gave me a wicked smile. He was calling my bluff.

While it wasn't convenient, I had to admit that wicked smile was very attractive.

I sighed and started walking towards class again. We both knew my dad would burst a kidney if he thought I really wanted to drop out of school.

Concentrating on American History class was next to impossible. Bits and pieces of my conversation with Josh kept intruding upon my thoughts, interjecting at inappropriate moments like an uninvited visitor walking into the house, tracking in mud, and bringing in a great big wet, smelly dog.

Study hall wasn't much better. I tried to finish my physics homework, but ended up spending most of the time staring out the window wondering how I was going to fix this.

By the time lunch rolled around, I knew I would have to tell Rhys what had happened. The thought made me feel sick inside – not the weasels-fighting-in-my-stomach kind of sick, but more of a nauseated feeling of hopelessness and despair. Just as bad as the weasels, if not worse.

It took me a while to figure out why I was dreading telling him so much, but it finally dawned on me. When Eric had been here, Rhys had always taken a back seat and seemed content to be in the background. With Josh back in the picture, I was afraid the same thing would happen again. I felt like I was stalking a bunny rabbit – too much noise and it would bolt. Did I really just compare Rhys to a rabbit?

When we sat down for lunch, I could see the look of expectation on Rhys' face.

"Are you ready to tell me what happened with Josh?" he asked. He smiled at me, and I took a deep breath, ready to spill it all. But before I could get more than a few words out, I saw Josh stand up from his usual table in the cafeteria and walk towards me.

Not exactly good timing.

"Hey, Madison," he said, and pulled up a chair next to me.

I glanced over at Rhys whose face had gone smooth and blank. No help there.

"Hi, Josh," I said. "What's up?"

"Well, I just wanted to invite you to come over and sit with us," he said. "Oh, and Rhys is welcome to come too," he said, but the invitation to Rhys was clearly an afterthought.

"I think I'm just going to stay here with Rhys," I said. "It will be easier for everyone that way."

Josh flashed me a smile. "I see. You're going to make me suffer for breaking up with you, aren't you? Well, don't worry. I'm here for the long haul. I'm going to keep trying every day and do whatever it takes to get you back. You just tell me what you want me to do and I'll do it. But for today, since you declined my invitation, I will leave you in peace."

And with that he headed back to his table. Several of the guys looked over and laughed, slapping Josh on the back in commiseration. The girls all had their heads together in a whispered huddle that was too soft for me to hear even during a pre-zerk.

Rhys watched Josh for a while before turning back to me. He was smiling, but it looked forced and didn't make it to his eyes. "I can't wait to hear this story."

There was no way to hide it now, so I told him everything. How Josh had confronted me, how I had accidentally placed a haze on him, and how he wanted to get back together with me again.

When I finished, Rhys looked thoughtful, playing with a cold French fry. "There's never a dull moment when you're around," he said. "A Berserker with Binder powers? I probably should have guessed."

"But what do I do?" I asked, a note of panic creeping into my voice. "How do I fix it?"

"Do you want it fixed?" Rhys asked. He met my eyes, asking me the hard question I wasn't sure I knew the answer to. "Now you can have your cake and eat it too. Hmm, perhaps a bad metaphor," he added when he saw the repulsed look on my face. "But the point is, you've been miserable since he broke up with you. Now you can keep Josh and be a Berserker. It's the best of both worlds."

"I suppose," I said, but there was no real enthusiasm in it. Yeah, Josh was cute, and I clearly had some unresolved feelings for him, but what would this do to any possibility of a relationship with Rhys? Was he angry, upset, or even slightly jealous? He didn't look like any of those things. He simply sat across from me looking beautiful and understanding.

How frustrating!

"If you want, when we get home we can ask Mallika about it, but I don't think there is much she is going to be able to do. I think at this point you're going to have to deal with this as a relationship, not a problem with Binder powers."

For the rest of lunch Josh continued to watch me from his table. Several times he caught me watching him back and motioned for me to come over. Each time I turned away, pretending I hadn't seen him.

I left lunch early to make sure that I didn't have another run-in with Josh. Rhys accompanied me to my locker to get my books for pre-calc. On the way, I saw Mrs. Abrams, my English teacher and the Drama coach plastering the walls with audition posters for the spring musical. I squealed when I saw what it was – Camelot. I had seen a production when I was much younger and had fallen in love with it. I even bought the Broadway soundtrack with Julie Andrews and Richard Burton.

Mrs. Abrams saw me peering over her shoulder and turned around, smiling at me.

"Are you going to try out, Madison?" she asked. "You are such a talented actress I would love to have you in the play. You should try out for Guinevere."

I blushed deeply at the complement. I had been in most of the plays since I had been in high school, but they were generally minor parts. I had never had the confidence to try out for a lead role.

"I don't know, Mrs. Abrams," I said. "I'm really busy these days, and I'm not sure I can make that kind of commitment."

"Well, you think about it," she said. "I hope to see you at auditions this Friday after school."

***

In the locker room while we changed for Gym class, Amy asked me about Josh.

"Are you and Josh back together?" she asked, her voice a whisper as she looked around surreptitiously.

"No," I said. "What gave you that idea?"

Amy gave an exasperated sigh. "I know you don't pay attention to the social happenings here, but you should at least be wired in on your own gossip."

I shrugged. "That's why I have you as a friend."

Amy beamed. "Yeah, it is." She leaned in close. "So the latest gossip is that Josh is trying to get back with you again. Everyone's talking about how he's gone back to his old self and invited you to sit with him at lunch. It's like he's been under a spell for the last several months and it was just broken."

I tried very hard to keep my face smooth and not show the panic I was feeling. Amy was a little too close to the truth for my comfort. She just had it reversed.

"Ginger is livid," Amy said. "Which is understandable since I'm pretty sure she's the witch who cast the spell." She paused, an exaggerated expression of thoughtfulness on her face. "Maybe I've got my words confused. I think the word I'm looking for to describe her actually starts with a B."

"Speaking of," I said. Ginger had just stormed in, her long red hair whipping around her, making her look even more fierce than usual. As she walked past she glared at me with an intense loathing that I hadn't seen from her for months. Clearly the intimidation had worn off.

"Come on," said Amy. "Let's get out of here before she

unsheathes her claws."

***

After school Rhys took me back to the Berserker house so I could talk with Mallika. He wanted to give us some privacy, so he and Kara left to run errands, leaving Mallika and me alone. We sat in the kitchen, on the padded stools in front of the large island. Mallika had made herself a cup of tea, and me a mug of hot chocolate – she knew it was my favorite.

As I spoke, Mallika listened quietly without interrupting until I had told her everything. When I was done she tapped her teacup, looking thoughtful.

"The evidence continues to mount in support of you being both a Berserker and Binder." Mallika sat up and took another sip. "My report to the council about your additional Binder abilities was met with skepticism. Most of the other Binders can't decide if I'm going senile, or concocting some scheme to manipulate them. But this new development moves us beyond just the ability to see Binder work. The fact that you are a Berserker and cast a haze without being trained means that the magic is changing, something that hasn't happened in a thousand years if not longer."

"But why?" I asked. "Why would Berserker powers change after so long?"

"I don't know that it's the Berserker powers that are changing Madison. I think this situation is particular to you and is happening *because* of you."

"Because of me?" I asked. "How can that be?"

"Because you are the child of a Berserker and a Binder, Madison. I believe that is what causes your powers to manifest differently than usual."

"But my dad said that other children had been born to Berserkers and Binders and that there was no genetic link?"

Mallika nodded. "He did say that, and he is right – after a fashion. I have done some investigating and it seems to me that there was one variable that was missing in the other cases."

I set down my mug. "What variable was that?"

"In the other cases where a child was born to a Berserker and Binder, there was never a death during the child's teenage years."

"What do you mean?"

Mallika cupped her hands around her tea. "There are only twelve Berserkers and twelve Binders at any given time. When one of them dies, another is chosen somewhere in the world. You already know this. The chosen is always a boy or girl in their early to mid teenage years. However, I discovered that in the cases of the other children of Berserker parents, there were no Berserker or Binder deaths while they were of age to receive the powers.

"It is entirely possible, and I would say even probable that the reason they never manifested powers like yours was because they missed their window of opportunity. By the time someone died and there was an opening, they were too old."

"What about Josh?" I asked. "If I am a Binder and really did cast a haze on him is there anything I can do to fix it?"

Mallika smiled at me. "My child, your problem is not with the haze. From everything you told me, you cast the haze perfectly. All you have done is to remove the reason for your break-up with Josh. Think about it from his perspective. He can no longer remember why you stopped dating. His feelings are now untainted by the fear and pain of that night." She reached out and put a comforting hand on mine. "It's up to you to decide how you want to handle the situation. Do you want to go back to the way things were with Josh, or are there other, uh, older men who may interest you instead?"

I blushed, and the room suddenly felt very warm. Was I just a completely open book that everyone could read, or was I cursed to be surrounded by exceptionally perceptive people?

Mallika stood and cleared our dishes. "Be happy Madison, not everyone is as loved as you are."

I knew there was truth in what she said, but somehow that didn't make my situation any easier.

***

As the week progressed Josh remained persistent. He left flowers in front of my locker, tried to walk with me between classes – which, since we didn't have any classes together, was rather difficult and caused him to be late for his own classes several times – and every day at lunch repeated his invitation to sit with him. He hadn't yet tried to sit with me and Rhys, but I wouldn't have put it past him.

I know there are girls who love to be chased. I wasn't one of those girls. While it was extremely flattering that Josh wanted me back, the net result was a massive spike in my stress level. I had difficulty sleeping – a rarity for me – and couldn't concentrate on my Berserker training. Rhys and I still practiced most days after school, but I felt like I had reached a plateau and wasn't getting any better.

Finally, on Thursday afternoon after a particularly mediocre sparring session in which Rhys repeatedly poked holes in my defense, I had an epiphany.

I wanted to be in the play.

Not just wanted – I *needed* to be in it. In the middle of all this stress, I needed to find something that was for me. Not for anyone else, not for the Berserkers, not for Rhys, or Josh, but me. I remembered how good it felt to be part of the cast and bond with the other actors. It was something I enjoyed, and I desperately needed something enjoyable in life right now.

I was going to try out for the play.

When I told Rhys, I thought he would object and tell me I should focus on my Berserker training and not waste my time on frivolous pursuits. I wouldn't have blamed him because that was exactly what the voice of duty was saying inside my head. Shouting was more like it. Like an angry drill sergeant, or worse – those guys who sell kitchen appliances on infomercials.

Instead he raised an eyebrow, but wisely did not try to talk me out of it. He took a moment and looked at me – I mean really looked at me. The kind of look that made my heart race, my face flush, and caused other embarrassing physical reactions.

"If it means that much to you then you should do it," he said. "It might be good for you. You haven't been yourself lately and maybe this will help."

I reached out and gave him a hug. "Thank you," I said.

"For what?"

"For understanding me."

***

Dad, on the other hand, wasn't quite as understanding.

"The Berserkers are out there hunting for Osadyn and instead of improving your skills, you want to be in a play?" he asked. "Is that really where your priorities are?"

I felt the beginnings of a spectacular fight brewing. Dad and I didn't fight often, but what we lacked in quantity we made up for in quality. I could already tell that this one was going to be one for the Montgomery family history books.

But before I could work up a good righteous indignation at Dad's comment, Rhys stepped in. He pulled Dad into his office and closed the door behind them.

I didn't want to eavesdrop, but I was upset, solidly in pre-zerk state. My hearing was too good to not hear them through the door, so I went onto the back porch and sat on a rocking chair, trying to calm down.

When Dad and Rhys came out ten minutes later, Dad looked

slightly sheepish and pulled me in for a hug.

"I'm sorry, Madison," he said. "If this is something you really want to do then you should do it. You have my full support."

It took all my effort not to let my jaw drop in surprise. Dad backed down on this? I looked over at Rhys, but he was carefully studying a lone bird hopping from branch to branch in the tree above. I didn't know what he had said to Dad, but I wanted him to teach that trick to me.

I squeezed Dad tight. "Thanks, Dad. You don't know how much this means to me!"

Dad pulled back and looked slightly embarrassed. "That's true. I didn't know how much it meant to you, and I should have. I've been so worried about you being a Berserker that I've forgotten that you're still a teenage girl. I'll do better in the future. I'm sorry."

***

During school Friday, I convinced Amy to try out with me. She had been in plays with me before and it was always more fun when she was part of the cast.

"I don't want a big part," she said. "Just a nice bit part that doesn't require much in the way of skill or talent – preferably non-speaking so I don't have to memorize any lines. Unless there's a kissing scene in this?"

That was my Amy.

***

Auditions were held in the auditorium right after school. Amy came to try out and Rhys tagged along for support – plus he was my ride home. During auditions, Mrs. Abrams typically asked each student to read an excerpt from the play. Those who were auditioning for major parts were also supposed to come prepared to sing a song. It didn't have to be from Camelot, but the audition announcement clearly stated that it would be to our advantage if we preformed one of the songs our part would sing.

I read a scene from Act two as Guinevere and Garry Crean read the part of King Arthur. I felt myself settle into the role of Guinevere and the words came easily for me. I felt alive and exhilarated. I hadn't realized how much I had missed being on the stage. It was liberating to take on another persona, even if it was just for a few minutes.

Then Josh walked into the auditorium.

What was he doing here? Josh was a jock and never even came to any of the plays, let alone attended the auditions. Apart from required assemblies, I didn't think I had ever seen him in the auditorium before.

I was so preoccupied with Josh's unexpected appearance that I stumbled on my next line, but quickly recovered and pushed him out of my thoughts. Right now I was Guinevere and there was no room for anyone in her life besides Arthur and Lancelot.

"Very good, Madison and Gary," said Mrs. Abrams when we had finished. She smiled at me as I exited the stage.

A few auditions later it was Amy's turn. She did a fantastic job. When she got off the stage I said, "You better be careful. If you keep this up you might get a major role."

She shrugged like it was no big deal, but the big grin on her face told the real story.

We sat back down in the audience a few rows behind Mrs. Abrams to watch the remaining readings and wait for the singing auditions.

When Mrs. Abrams called out "Josh Lancaster, for the part of Lancelot." I couldn't decide whether to laugh or cry. I must admit that the thought of big, strong jock Josh Lancaster trying out for the school play made me more inclined toward the laughter option. Leave it to him to think acting was easy and that he could just step in and do it without any training. I would enjoy watching him flop. It would serve him right.

But there was no flop. To say I was shocked wouldn't be a strong enough sentiment. It would be more like jaw-droppingly-blown-away. Who knew the boy could act?

If that was not enough of the unexpected for one day, three auditions later Mrs. Abrams read "Rhys Owen, for the part of Lancelot."

I turned to face him. "Are you serious? When did you decide to try out?"

He shrugged. "About ten minutes ago." He turned and walked onto the stage.

When Mrs. Abrams selected a part for Rhys to read, he merely glanced at the scene and then set the script down. We watched in amazement as he recited every line word for word – no mistakes or hesitation. When had he had time to memorize the script? As if it wasn't impressive enough that he had the part memorized, he also managed to bring Lancelot to life on the stage. Watching him speak, I could almost imagine him as the legendary warrior ready to devote himself to King Arthur's cause.

When he finished everyone applauded. We hadn't done that for the other tryouts, but none of them had the part memorized or delivered the lines so flawlessly.

On the way back to his seat, Rhys walked past Josh, who didn't look too happy at this turn of events. He glowered and slumped back in his seat with his arms folded, a grim look on his face. He was a competitor and it was obvious he didn't like to lose. And he would be hard pressed to get the part after Rhys' performance.

"That was great," I whispered to Rhys once he sat back down. "Where did you learn to act like that?"

"One of the advantages of living a long time," he said, "is that you tend to pick up this kind of thing."

Once all the acting try-outs were complete it was time for the singing portion. When I was called to the stage I sang "The Simple Joys of Maidenhood" where Guinevere sings about the unfairness of her prearranged marriage. It was one of my favorites – poignant and humorous at the same time. I had sung this song a thousand times growing up, and when I got on stage I tried to imagine myself as Guinevere, caught between her duty to her people and her desire to live her own life.

I could relate to the girl.

With the first note I knew I had knocked this out of the park. I hit every note, nailed every word, and really *felt* the song.

When it was over I felt flush with excitement. I took a quick bow and hurried off back to my seat to watch the other performers.

Josh chose to sing "C'Est Moi" one of Lancelot's best songs. Once again I was surprised at how well he did. His voice was nowhere near strong or deep enough to do the song real justice, but it wasn't really fair for me to compare him to Robert Goulet on the Broadway recording.

Rhys was the last singer. When Mrs. Abrams called him up, he walked very slowly and deliberately to the stage. As he walked I could almost see him changing, growing older, more mature. When he stood on stage and faced the audience, he almost seemed like a different person.

I had always considered myself to be a good actress, but Rhys could have been a professional. His ability to take on a persona through expression and subtle mannerisms was amazing.

And then he sang.

I hadn't exactly expected him to be horrible, but I certainly didn't expect him to be good. And he wasn't just good. He was why-wasn't-he-a-recording-star good. He'd selected "If Ever I Would Leave You", the song Lancelot sings to Guinevere expressing his undying love for her. His voice was breathtaking, pounding out the deep notes and soaring on the high ones.

His eyes met mine, and as he sang I felt the words deep within me. After a moment, my chest felt constricted and I realized that I had been so entranced that I had actually stopped breathing. I forced myself to relax and breathe normally.

There was silence when he finished. We were all too stunned to do anything. By the time we had recovered enough to think of applauding, he had already climbed down from the stage.

"Thank you, Rhys," said Mrs. Abrams. "Thank you all for participating. I will take the weekend to go over my notes and Monday morning I will post the cast list outside my classroom door. Have a wonderful weekend!"

***

Saturday morning began with the doorbell ringing at ten o'clock. I had spent most of Friday night obsessing over the auditions and what the cast list would be on Monday, and consequently didn't get to sleep until about two in the morning.

When I heard the doorbell, I woke up just long enough to turn over and go back to bed. But more blissful sleep was denied me when I heard a knock at my door.

"I'm still asleep," I said.

Mom opened the door and poked her head in. "You have a visitor," she said.

"Already? Tell them I'm still sleeping." I turned and put the pillow over my head.

"Ok," said Mom in an overly casual tone. "I'll just tell Rhys you're sleeping."

She started to close the door, but I sat up and motioned for her to stop. Actually, I just sort of waved my hand frantically while I yawned, but Mom got the point.

"Tell him I'll be down in a minute."

Mom gave me a knowing smile. "Will do, sweetie."

I got up and walked over to the mirror to inspect the damage. I couldn't just go down stairs as I was, but I didn't have time to fully get ready. I remembered Amy saying that anytime you met up with a guy and it wasn't a planned date, the trick was to look good while making it look like you put no effort into it.

A few strokes of the brush tamed my hair enough to be presentable. I brushed my teeth just enough to get rid of my morning breath – not like he was going to kiss me, but it didn't hurt to be prepared – and I switched out of my old sweats and into the cute satin pajamas I never wore because I kept sliding out of bed.

When I got downstairs, Rhys was sitting at the kitchen table with my mom.

"Madison was fantastic," he said. "I'm sure she'll get the part."

Rhys saw me come in and quickly stood up in an oddly formal gesture. What was up with that? I'd seen him practically every day for the past four months – was that really all it had been? – and he didn't usually act like this. Something was different.

"Don't let him be modest, Mom," I said as I sat down at the table. "Rhys was the star of the auditions. I was good, but he should be on

Broadway."

"Really?" said Mom, arching an eyebrow. "That's high praise coming from Madison."

Rhys shrugged. "I've been in a few plays before, but Madison has a natural gift for theater."

Mom put a hand on mine. "I hope you get the part," she said and then stood up. "Well, I have a few things I need to go do. It was nice talking with you, Rhys."

And with that she left, leaving Rhys and I alone together. This was not the first time we had been alone together, but something about Rhys was different – he seemed nervous.

"So," I said, breaking the awkward silence that had fallen when Mom left. "What's up? More Berserker training?"

Rhys looked down at hands. "Not training," he said. "I was just thinking that maybe we could go out and do something together today. You know, to take your mind off of the wait for the posted cast list." He looked up at me hopefully.

It took all my Berserker training to prevent me from pre-zerking and giving away my excitement. Was he asking me out? On a date? I bit my tongue to keep from squealing with excitement – great to do with girlfriends, not so impressive in front of the boy himself.

"Sure," I said, trying to sound calm. "What did you have in mind?"

"I have a couple of ideas," he said.

My smile faded slightly. I sure hoped this wasn't going to be one of those times when the guy asked me what I wanted to do and had nothing planned. I hated that.

He saw my look of concern and smiled. "Don't worry," he said. "It will be fun, I promise. Dress warm."

***

When we pulled into the parking lot of the ice skating rink I wanted to cry. I had gone ice skating twice in my life, but both times ended up injured. As a result, I had sworn it off several years ago and hadn't been back since.

"I don't think this is such a good idea," I said. I couldn't bring myself to look at Rhys – partly because I was afraid I was going to hurt his feelings, and partly because I was embarrassed for being such a baby about not wanting to ice skate.

Rhys reached out and gently turned my face up so I was looking at him, his face mere inches from mine. His eyes drew me in.

"Trust me," he said. "You will love this."

"No," I said vaguely. I found it extremely difficult to concentrate with him that close to me. I had a very rational story with examples and proof of why ice skating and I didn't mix very well, but I couldn't remember all the details at the moment – would he just lean over and kiss me, for crying out loud!

"No?" Rhys pulled back slightly, breaking my stupor. "What do you have against ice skating?"

"I always get hurt," I said, "or hurt someone else."

With a laugh, Rhys climbed out and opened my door, helping me out of the Range Rover. "You're not the same girl you were," he said. "This will be a whole new experience."

Rhys reached out and took my hand, pulling me toward the entrance of the skating rink. I felt a tingle at his touch, and I reluctantly let him lead me into the skating rink.

We got our rental skates and sat down on large blocks to put them on. I laced mine up as tightly as I could because I remembered how difficult it was to keep my ankles from wobbling. How did I end up back here again? Oh, the dumb things girls did for guys they liked!

Fortunately this early in the day the rink was practically empty, just a few people skating around on the ice. I tentatively took a couple of steps with my skates and immediately grabbed the rail when we got out onto the ice.

Rhys laughed at the look of panic on my face. "You're a Berserker now," he said. "You have better balance and coordination than any human could possibly have. If you give it a chance you'll find you can do this as easily as walking."

"Trust me, I find ways to mess that up," I said, still not letting go of the rail.

Rhys shrugged and took off. With smooth powerful movements, he accelerated and began zipping around the rink. He even threw in a couple of jumps and turns. It was truly an amazing sight. He looked like he had been born to do this, moving with the quick grace of an Olympic figure skater.

Talk about intimidating. Not only was I going to look like an idiot on the ice, but next to Rhys, I was going to look like an even bigger one than usual.

It was time to get this over with.

I took a deep breath, pushed my panic back, and tried to find my balance. Immediately I noticed that I wasn't having any trouble keeping my ankles straight, so that was an improvement. Hesitantly, I let go of the rail and managed to keep my balance. I made a few experimental pushes with my skates and found myself gliding across the ice at an unexpected speed.

I pushed harder and found my rhythm. After a few minutes of experimenting, I had gotten the hang of it and could maneuver around the rink at will.

Rhys came over and skated next to me. "How's it going?" he asked.

For the first time since I had found out we were going to ice skate, I smiled. "Not as bad as I thought."

With a grin, Rhys took my hand and skated alongside me. Hand in hand we skated together, simply enjoying each other's company.

After a few minutes, Rhys began to speed up. To my surprise, I discovered I had no trouble keeping up with him. At one point he tightened his grip on my hand and turned hard so that we spun together in a circle, faster and faster. Instead of getting dizzy, I felt a thrill of excitement – this was fun!

For the next several hours we raced and played, leaped and turned. Rhys had been right, this was nothing like the embarrassing clumsiness of my last skating experience. I smiled at the looks of amazement the other skaters gave us as we played. At one point I jumped and spun around five times before landing. My sensitive hearing heard several people gasp in amazement and whisper to each other.

When we were finally done, Rhys went to take back our rented skates, and a little girl around five years old came up to me with a piece of paper and a pen. "Can I have your autograph?" she asked.

I flushed with embarrassment. "Sweetie, why would you want my autograph?"

The little girl shrugged. "My Mom said you must be an Olympic skater."

"I'm sorry to disappoint you, sweetheart, but I'm just a normal person. I'm not famous, and I've never been to the Olympics."

The girl looked up at me with such a pathetic look that I felt like I had just taken away Christmas from her. "But if you still want my autograph," I said, "you can have it."

"Yea!" She handed me the paper, and I signed my name to it. She grinned, took the autograph and skipped back to her mother, waving it excitedly.

"That was very sweet," said Rhys, who had apparently watched the entire exchange.

"Yeah, well, I've got to keep my fan happy," I said. "All one of her."

Rhys reached up and brushed a strand of hair from in front of my face. "I think you will find you have more fans than just her," he said.

I took a deep, calming breath. Was he saying what I thought he was saying? This wasn't the first time he had hinted at a deeper interest than mere friendship. But every time things started to get serious, he would suddenly turn away and the moment would end.

As if my mental frustration were an audible cue, he abruptly dropped his hand and looked away, a pained look on his face. I wanted to bang my head on the ice in frustration, or better yet, bang Rhys' head on the ice until he stopped being so confusing.

***

By the time Monday came around, I was pretty much a basket case. I had gone from extreme confidence that I would get the part, to certainty that my audition was awful and that I was a terrible actress, to confidence once again. I had then repeated that cycle at least once per hour during the entire weekend.

I met Amy at her locker before school started. "Are you ready to see the cast list?" I asked.

She was. She grabbed my arm and together we ran down the hall to Mrs. Abrams' room.

There were several other people in front of the pieces of paper pinned to the bulletin board outside her classroom. I tried to be patient as I waited for the people in front of me to read the list, but I was practically shaking with excitement when it was my turn.

I spotted Amy's name first. She was one of Guinevere's ladies in waiting. I pointed it out to her and we squealed and hugged. But not for too long – I still needed to see whether I'd gotten a part. Turning my attention back to the paper, I read through the names to find that

I had been cast as Guinevere.

Now Amy and I began to celebrate in earnest. We squealed again and jumped up and down with excitement. I knew it wasn't very dignified and that I probably looked like an idiot, but I was too excited to really care.

"Who are the leading men?" asked Amy. We consulted the list again.

I sighed with relief when I read that Rhys had gotten the part of Lancelot. I must admit that I was looking forward to spending more time with him, and not just in combat training. There were some passionate scenes between Lancelot and Guinevere and I was definitely hoping it might transfer to a little offstage romance.

But my relief was short-lived. I scanned the other parts and saw who had been cast as King Arthur: Josh Lancaster.

Well, this was going to be awkward.

CHAPTER 4

THE TEST OF A BINDER

R ehearsals turned out to be just as awkward as I had anticipated. Fortunately there were no actual kissing scenes in the play, or I might have quit just to avoid the sheer awkwardness.

Rhys accepted the situation gracefully. I could sense he wasn't thrilled about Josh playing King Arthur, but he managed to be polite and respectful.

Josh, however, wasn't quite as good at keeping his feelings to himself. He maintained a semblance of civility when they were on stage together, but offstage he never acknowledged Rhys' presence except to glare at him.

To make matters worse, Josh dumped Ginger the day he got the part and specifically told her – or so Amy told me – that he was still in love with me and wanted to get back together.

Ginger hadn't liked me before. Now she loathed me.

Relationship awkwardness aside, I enjoyed the rehearsals. Rhys and I practiced every day after rehearsal, and I had my part memorized in less than two weeks – ok, I actually cheated and read through the part while I was pre-zerking, but what good are superpowers if you can't use them to make your life easier?

As far as I could tell, Rhys never even opened his script. Somehow he had memorized his part before auditions. Apart from the blocking and determining where we delivered our lines on the stage, Rhys could have stood up and performed the whole thing on day one.

His quick mastery of the part clearly irritated Josh, who had a much harder time memorizing the part of King Arthur. He often had to refer back to the script or get prompted for his next line. This was most obvious when they were on stage together and Rhys would feed Josh his next line. Josh would grind his teeth and Rhys would simply wait patiently for him to deliver the next line, pretending he couldn't see the smoldering fury in Josh's expression.

The rehearsal schedule meant that my Berserker training had to be done later in the evening and was often cut somewhat short. Dad clearly didn't like it, but he reluctantly admitted that cutting back on the training didn't seem to be affecting my skills – too much.

Between school, rehearsals, and Berserker training, I spent the majority of my day with Rhys – something that I certainly wasn't going to complain about. I loved spending any time with him that I could. He still confused me to no end, switching off between showing interest in me and coldly distancing himself – sometimes both within less than a minute – but I could feel the emotion between us when we were on stage.

Our scenes together as a forbidden relationship felt so real to me that when I spoke the lines of Guinevere, I felt them as Madison. The desire to leave everything behind and spend my life with this one man was at times almost dizzying.

My parts with Josh were fine. He clearly enjoyed the opportunity to interact with me and took every advantage he could to get close. He took his time, releasing me slowly when he was supposed to take my hand or pull me in for an embrace. I endured it patiently and watched Rhys for his reaction to Josh's advances.

Unfortunately Rhys maintained an outer façade of calmness that gave me no insight into his feelings. I just couldn't understand that boy. It was like he was two separate people. When we were alone together I would get a glimpse of the funny, warm, and charming Rhys – what I was starting to think of as the real Rhys. But just as it would seem like things were progressing, the real Rhys would be replaced by some standoffish doppelganger who treated me like his kid sister.

Ginger was less reserved about her feelings. She didn't confront me openly – she seemed reluctant to face me after the basketball incident – but she tried all sorts of passive methods to make me miserable. Unfortunately for her, I no longer cared that much about the things like social status and popularity, so Ginger's efforts to get back at me were less effective than she had hoped.

For example, the weekend after Josh broke up with her, Ginger and her friends had toilet papered my house. Rhys and I were home at the time. Instead of rushing out to stop her, I grabbed some extra toilet paper rolls from the bathroom closet, slipped outside, and then tapped Ginger on the shoulder offering them to her. I think I sort of took the fun out of it because they dropped the rolls they still had and slunk away.

***

Several weeks into rehearsals, something happened that temporarily took my mind off of Rhys, Josh, and Ginger.

When we arrived home from practice Dad was waiting for me on the front porch. I could tell by how stiffly he sat in the chair that something was wrong.

"Hey, Dad. What's going on?"

Dad's gaze shifted from me to Rhys and then back. "I just got a call from Mallika," he said. "She asked me to have you come to the Berserker house as quickly as possible."

"Why?"

His mouth tightened into a thin line. "The Binder's Conclave is here with the Sarolt stone," he said.

It had finally happened. After months of waiting, the Conclave finally sent the stone Mallika had requested. Part of me was excited, but in some ways the announcement was anti-climactic because I doubted the stone could tell us anything we didn't already know.

What I didn't understand is why Dad looked so upset about it. His grim expression while he relayed the message had made me think someone had died.

I dropped off my backpack and climbed back into the Range Rover with Rhys. As he drove to the Berserker house, he too looked tense and gripped the steering wheel hard enough that his knuckles turned white.

"What's going on?" I asked. "Nobody seems too happy about this."

Rhys shrugged. "It's nothing, really. Just more of the politics of the Berserker world."

I managed to keep my groan inside. Being the new kid was frustrating enough without the Berserkers trying to protect me all the time. I wanted to grab his shoulders, and yell at him to stop being so overprotective. Instead, I managed a tight smile and said, "Well, fill me in before we get there." Boys could be so dense sometimes.

Rhys let out a breath and relaxed his grip on the steering wheel. "It's not a big deal, really," he said. "There are just some power struggles between the Berserkers and the Binders."

"Really?" I asked. "You and Mallika seem to get along. And Kara and Aata, well, they got along fine until their relationship went nuclear."

"True," said Rhys. "The Binders who are paired one to one with the Berserkers for each of the five Havocs get along fine with their Berserkers. It's the seven Binders who together bind Verenix that are the problem."

"How so?"

"Like I said, it's not a big deal, so don't read too much into this.

There are just... disagreements about who is in charge. The Berserkers want to do things their own way, and the Binders think they should be the ones giving orders. They created the Binder Conclave and seem to think that it should make all the decisions about where the Berserkers go and when. The seven Berserkers who are part of Verenix's binding don't mind because, well, they're more interested in showing off and one-upping each other than actually capturing Havocs."

"Don't they want the Havocs bound?"

"They want them bound. They just don't think it's their job. As long as Verenix is bound, they consider their duty completed. They each take their turn going into hiding for six months and that's it. The rest of the time they're about pushing the limits of their powers to have fun."

We pulled up to the gate of the house and Rhys punched in the code. As we drove up the driveway, I noticed an unfamiliar black BMW out front.

Inside we found Mallika and Kara sitting in the living room with two older ladies. Kara practically jumped to her feet as we came in, her mascara slightly smudged as if she had been crying. She put her arm around me rather protectively and brought me over to the visitors, one of whom had stood.

"Madison, this is Naki." She gestured to a rather tall woman. She wore a white scarf decorated with bright yellow flowers wrapped over the top of her head and draped around her shoulders. Her skin was a deep brown and heavily wrinkled.

Naki smiled and inclined her head. "It is a pleasure to finally meet you in person, Madison," she said. "I have heard so much about you."

Next, Kara gestured to a petite woman wearing a black dress with a red and gold shawl around her shoulders. Her features were Asian and her skin was practically flawless, a few wrinkles being the only hint that she might be older than she looked.

"And this is Sunee. Both of them are from the Binder Conclave."

Sunee's expression was completely flat, without a hint of emotion. She nodded to me, but did not speak.

Mallika, however, stood up and gave me a hug. "It's good to see you again, Madison. Between your play and training, I don't see nearly enough of you." She gave me a warm, reassuring smile and then gestured at an empty chair. "Please have a seat."

I sat in one of the overstuffed chairs and for several moments no one spoke. The entire situation felt extremely uncomfortable, and just being in the company of these women made me feel like a preschooler sitting in on a college lecture.

Naki let out a laugh, which was so unexpected that it made me jump. I caught sight of Sunee and noticed the corners of her lips twitch. Was that a smile? I felt really confused about what was going on here.

"This is far too formal," said Naki, a large grin making her eyes crinkle. She stood up and reached out a hand to me, helping me out of the deep cushioning of my overstuffed chair. "Let's adjourn to the kitchen and make this more casual."

We sat around the large oak table off to the side of the kitchen. Naki placed a hand on Kara's and gave it a small squeeze. "Kara, dear, would you please make us something to drink? I would like some tea, and," she peered closely at me, "perhaps some hot cocoa for Madison."

Kara immediately stood up and began making preparations. It was the most obedient I had ever seen her. What was it about these two that made people want to obey them?

"Neat trick," I said. "How did you know I liked cocoa?"

Naki gave me a knowing smile. "I make it my business to know about the Binders, Madison," she said.

"And I mentioned it to her earlier when we discussed possible refreshments," Mallika added.

"Oh, stop giving away an old woman's secrets." Naki smiled and there was something in the way she looked at Mallika that made me think she was much more serious than she was letting on.

We spent the next few minutes on small talk, until Kara had brought over the tea and cocoa. That seemed to be Naki's cue to get down to business.

"The Sarolt stone is the method we use to identify Binders and Berserkers," she said. "We rarely need it for Berserkers since it is generally quite obvious whether one can Berserk or not – that glow is a bit of a giveaway, isn't it?"

I nodded. That was very true – 'zerking was rather distinctive.

"Sunee here is the keeper of the stone, and has brought it with her so that we can test you." Naki nodded at Sunee, who reached into a pocket and pulled out a small wooden box painted with bright blue, gold, and red symbols.

She opened the box to reveal an oblong shaped stone, roughly cut with hard angles and edges. The stone was the opposite of shiny – it actually sucked in the light around it, creating a strange, shadowy, aura.

"This is the Sarolt stone," said Sunee, speaking for the first time. Her voice was high and melodious, a contrast from what I had expected given her apparently dour nature. "This stone has been passed down from Binder to Binder since the great beginning. It is our greatest treasure."

I stared at the stone, transfixed. There was something about its inky blackness and the way it seemed to swallow the ambient light that both fascinated and repulsed me. I had the overwhelming desire to touch it.

Seemingly of its own accord, my hand lifted from the table and reached out towards the stone. Immediately, Sunee pulled the box back and snapped it shut, jarring me out of my reverie.

"Do not touch," she said, giving me an accusatory glare, as if I had just tried to spray graffiti on a priceless piece of art.

Only after both my hands were back in my lap did Sunee open the box again and set it on the table. Obviously, she took the protection of this stone very seriously. The word fanatical came to mind.

"I believe our first order of business," said Naki, "is to see if you are indeed a Binder. Mallika has told us about your special circumstances, and that without training you have cast a haze. That is truly impressive."

What I seemed to remember Mallika telling me was that no one believed I was both a Binder and a Berserker. Either something had happened to change their opinion – and I couldn't think of anything that might have done that – or this experiment was expected to fail and discredit Mallika.

"That's right," I said, more confidently than I actually felt. If this failed, it wouldn't be from my lack of trying.

"Excellent," said Naki. If she wanted me to fail, she sure was hiding it well. "Now, what I need you to do, Madison, is to cast the beginning – and just the beginning mind you, no one wants to lose their memory – of a haze."

That seemed simple enough. I looked over at Mallika and she nodded her approval.

I closed my eyes and thought back to what I had felt when I had cast the haze on Josh – the overwhelming desire for him to forget, the feeling of reaching out and pushing that desire out of me.

Blue mist sprayed out of my hand in a large cloud that sent everyone at the table scrambling to avoid touching it. Considering the age of Mallika and Naki, they both moved much faster than I would have expected.

While everyone jumped out of the way, the Sarolt stone lit up with a bright red light, casting strange purplish shadows through the blue mist.

"Sorry," I said, helping Naki back to her feet. "I don't have much control yet."

But Naki didn't seem upset. Quite the opposite in fact, she was practically giddy with excitement.

"That was wonderful!" she said once we were all back at the table. "Such force and volume! I've never seen its like, have you Sunee?"

Sunee shook her head. "I have not." She still didn't smile, but she appeared a bit shaken, and looked at me rather warily.

"So, there can be no question about it," Naki said. "The stone has verified it – you are a Binder." She paused and looked at all of us, beaming. "Now, Mallika tells us that you are also the first female Berserker in history. Is that correct?" Her smile was bigger now. I was still torn about her motives – I couldn't tell if she really was excited to see what I could do, or if she was just hoping to embarrass Mallika.

"Yes," I said. "I am also a Berserker."

"You have then actually had a full Berserking?" Sunee asked.

"Yes," I said, doing my best to keep a measure of patience in my voice. I couldn't really blame them if they doubted. I still remembered the shocked looks on the Berserkers' faces when they realized I was a girl. "Would you like a demonstration?"

"Absolutely," said Naki. She turned to Kara and put a hand on her arm. "I haven't been this excited in years!"

Unlike my Binder skills, my Berserker skills were much better honed. In an instant, I had triggered a full 'zerk and began glowing.

The reaction of Naki and Sunee was appropriately gratifying. Sunee watched with wide eyes while Naki leaned back, a hand covering her mouth in surprise.

The Sarolt stone glowed a deep navy blue and began to pulse with the light glowing brighter, then dimmer, over and over.

"Remarkable," said Naki. "A Binder and a Berserker in one. We truly are living in unusual times."

I stopped 'zerking, and the stone returned to its sucking blackness.

Mallika folded her arms and fixed Naki with an expectant look.

Letting out a sigh, Naki said, "I apologize for doubting you, Mallika. You were right and the girl really is something never before seen."

"She really is something special," said Mallika, giving me a wink.

"Well, if everything you've been telling us is true," said Naki, "and I'm sure it is," she added upon seeing the looks from Mallika and Kara, "then what I would like very much to see this, what do you call it, pre-zerk. A useful ability I must say. The capacity to heighten one's senses and access some of one's power without the visible signs of a full Berserking is quite remarkable. Could we see a demonstration?"

With a shrug, I tapped into my emotions and pre-zerked with hardly any effort.

The results were spectacular. The stone glowed a brilliant sky blue and sent rays of that same blue light flashing across the ceiling. The light bounced around the room, almost playfully, as if it were alive.

Sunee gasped and closed the lid. The light winked out, leaving the room feeling darker than before.

Naki clapped her hands excitedly. "Oh, that was spectacular!" she said.

"Is she the one?" said Sunee. It was very soft, hardly more than a whisper, but I was still pre-zerking and heard it quite clearly.

Naki's excitement vanished, her eyes flashing with anger. "Do not bring up Conclave business outside of the circle," she whispered back.

Sunee stared at Naki for a moment, and then bowed her head in submission.

"What Conclave business is that?" asked Mallika, arching an eyebrow.

Naki stood. "It means exactly what it says. Conclave business that can only be discussed in the privacy of the circle." She pushed back from the table and motioned for Sunee to do the same.

"I believe it's time for us to go now," she said.

Mallika held up a hand. "Before you go, do I have permission to teach Madison the ways of the Binders?" she asked.

Sunee and Naki looked at each other a moment before Naki answered. "The Sarolt stone has spoken," she said. "There can be no doubt that she is both a Binder and a Berserker. As such, she needs to be trained as a Binder. You have the Conclave's permission."

And with that, Naki and Sunee embraced Kara and Mallika, kissing them on the cheeks before leaving.

Once they were in their BMW and driving away, Kara let out a deep breath.

"I'm glad that's over with," she said. "Those two make me nervous. What was Naki talking about at the end about Conclave business? I didn't catch what Sunee said."

"Me neither," said Mallika. "But I would really like to know."

"I heard," I said. "I was still pre-zerking. She asked if I was 'the one'. Do you know what that means?"

"No," said Mallika. She cocked her head to the side, looking thoughtful. "But I intend to find out."

CHAPTER 5

BEACHES, CONFESSIONS, AND SPOONS

O ver the next two weeks, thoughts of Naki and Sunee were driven from my mind by sheer scheduling. Between school, play practice, Berserker training, and now Binder training, I had no time for anything that didn't require my immediate attention.

Mallika and Kara took turns teaching me basic control techniques, much like the practice that had helped me learn how to 'zerk on command. While not physically exhausting, my Binder training was mentally and emotionally draining. Each night after it was over I would fall into bed, lucky to remain conscious long enough to change out of my clothes.

Play practice continued to be awkward. Josh had finally learned his part well enough that Rhys couldn't annoy him by prompting him with his lines, but off stage they might as well have been a couple of dogs circling and defending their territory – me.

As stressful as it was, the one positive factor was Rhys'

increasingly visible interest in me – at least when Josh was around. When we were alone he still had a tendency to keep me at arm's length, but it was better than nothing.

A few days before the final dress rehearsal, Amy and I sat in the audience watching Josh and Rhys practice a scene onstage.

Amy leaned over to me and said, "What's it like having two hot guys both wanting you?"

"It's a lot like taking out my own appendix without anesthesia," I said. "Only less fun."

Amy rolled her eyes. "Really?" she said. "It's that bad?" She was clearly unconvinced.

"Worse."

"Worse than having no one interested in you?"

Now that question made me think. In some ways the stress involved was worse, but I also remembered what it had been like when I was pining after Josh with no hope of requital.

"Different, but equally sucky," I finally said.

"So which one do you like more, Josh or Rhys?" Amy asked. She watched the stage, deliberately not looking at me. I could tell she was up to something.

"What's going on?" I asked.

Amy tore her eyes away from the stage and gave me an innocent look. "What do you mean?"

Now it was my turn to roll my eyes. "Don't give me those doe-eyes. I've been your best friend too long to fall for that one."

Amy shrugged and leafed through her script. "I just wanted to see if you really liked both of them."

"Well I don't. At least I don't think I do." Did I? "I know I like Rhys, but this whole thing with Josh has become awkward…" I trailed off. It suddenly dawned on me what Amy was hinting at. "Why? Do you like one of them?" I asked. A very unwanted and ridiculous pang of jealousy flashed through me.

Amy closed her script. "Me and every other female on the planet. Oh, come on," she said when she saw my look of shock. "Nearly every girl in school likes one of those two guys. I just wanted to know which one you liked so I could stay away from him."

I didn't know whether to laugh, scream, or cry.

Closing my eyes, I took several deep breaths. The problem was that I wasn't sure what I wanted. Well, I did. I liked Rhys, and I was pretty sure he liked me too. But something seemed to be keeping him from taking that next step into a real relationship. Until I figured out what that was, it didn't seem like we were going to have any real progress. If I couldn't be with Rhys, did I want to be with Josh instead? Was that fair to him? To only want to be with him because I couldn't be with the guy I *really* liked? Wouldn't that be leading him on?

"I really don't know, Amy," I said. "This is unfamiliar territory for me. I'm used to pining after hot guys, not being the object of a Neanderthal tug-of-war. I can't really get mad at Josh because he's such a nice guy, but what I really want is for Rhys to just tell me how he feels." By the end of this my voice had gotten louder. I realized that several people were looking at us.

Amy made some shushing gestures and once everyone had turned back to watch Rhys and Josh, she leaned in and whispered, "Well, if there ever is a clear victor in the tug-of-war contest, let me know so I can start comforting the loser." She gave me her most conspiratorial smile, and I couldn't help but smile back.

That was my Amy.

***

In Binder training that evening Mallika taught me how to weave a snare. Kara came along to help.

We met in the hidden training room at my house, which I was now coming to think of as my second bedroom given all the time I spent in there.

"The key to weaving a snare is patience," said Mallika. "Have you ever done any knitting or crocheting?"

I nodded. It had been a few years, but back when I had plenty of free time on the weekends, Mom had taught Amy and me the basics. I had made a few scarves and even attempted a pair of socks, although they ended up looking more like misshapen baked potatoes.

"Good," Mallika said, "because you are going to weave the binding tendrils together to create a rope strong enough to hold a Havoc. A basic knowledge of any kind of weaving makes the process much easier.

"First we need to help you generate the initial tendrils." She went on to explain the rather complicated theory behind it.

"It sometimes helps to see it done by someone else when you are first learning," said Kara. She raised her hands and thin black tendrils oozed out of her finger tips, sinking towards the floor. As they grew in length, they wove together in a simple braided pattern.

"Okay, Madison," said Mallika. "Try to feel what she's doing and see if you can do the same. Don't be frustrated if nothing happens, this isn't an easy skill to learn."

I concentrated. Mallika was right, I could *feel* the snare Kara was weaving. I took in a deep breath and pushed.

Thick, black cables shot out of my fingers, flying across the room and rebounding off the walls. I jumped back and stopped the snare, the ends of it flying away from me as I released my mental hold.

Silence dominated the room. Mallika and Kara were wide eyed with shock.

"I'm sorry," I said. "This happened before, and I don't know what I'm doing wrong."

Kara started to laugh. "You don't know what you did wrong?" she said, her Scottish accent was difficult to understand through her laughter. "You didn't do a thing wrong. That was brilliant!"

"When did you try this before?" Mallika asked.

"During the solstice," I said. "You two were working so hard and I thought I would give it a try to see if I could help. But instead of making a useful weave, mine just sort of flew out all over the place."

"Can you do that again?" Mallika asked. "Perhaps a bit slower?"

"I'll try." I closed my eyes and concentrated on pushing the feeling outward. Once again thick, black cables came out of my fingertips, but this time they emerged more slowly.

Mallika reached out and held one of the cables, examining it closely. It felt strange having her touch it. I could somehow sense her through the cable – feel her touch.

"You never cease to amaze me, Madison," Mallika said, releasing the cable. "Never in all my time as a Binder have I seen anything like this."

"Is that in a 'I've never seen anything so incredible' kind of sense or more of a 'I've never seen anyone mess up a snare that badly' kind of sense?"

"Definitely the incredible one," Kara said. "What you did completely changes the game."

"Changes the game? What do you mean?" I asked.

Kara looked at Mallika in disbelief and then back at me. "Didn't you see what you just did? You cast the thickest snare I've ever even heard of. And the way it shot out of you was amazing."

"What Kara is trying to say," said Mallika, "is that your snare was so thick you wouldn't need to weave it to make it strong enough to hold a Havoc. You also created it much more quickly than any Binder we have seen, which means you could potentially create a snare strong enough to hold a Havoc on demand. There would be no need to weave it first and try to lure the Havoc inside."

We spent the next hour testing how fast I could produce a snare and learning how to control the direction of the individual tendrils. I may not have had to weave the tendrils into a rope, but I would still need to maneuver them to tie up the Havoc. Otherwise it would simply walk away from my jumble of cables.

Maneuvering the cables turned out to be much harder than I expected. By the end of the lesson, I could make them rise a few feet into the air, but not much beyond that.

"Don't worry," said Mallika, giving me a good-bye hug. "That comes with practice. And believe me, you will have plenty of that."

***

When Rhys drove me home on Friday, I could tell that something was on his mind. Rhys was never what I would call "chatty" on the best of days, but he seemed even quieter than usual.

"Are you okay?" I asked.

Rhys turned to me, his expression confused. "I think so," he said. "Why?"

"No reason," I said. "You just seem quiet today."

For some reason my comment made him blush. "Well, I've just been doing some thinking," he said.

"About what?"

"Nothing really," he said. Then in a too-casual tone of voice he said, "So, do you have any plans tomorrow?"

My pulse quickened, and I felt a thrill of excitement. I took a few deep breaths, doing my best not to let my emotions run wild and slip into a pre-zerk.

"Just practice with you," I said. "Why?"

"Well, I was just thinking that... I mean you've been working so hard with this play and Berserker training and now Binder training that I thought maybe tomorrow you should take the day off."

I should take the day off? My heart sunk, and I snapped back to reality. Not *we* – just me. He wasn't asking me out; he was trying to get away from me. But why? Was he sick of me already? Maybe I had done something to offend him, or even worse – maybe he was interested in another girl and already had a date planned.

"Okay," I said, trying to keep my voice more cheerful than I felt. "If that's what you want. Maybe Amy and I can do something together."

A look of panic crossed Rhys face, and his eyes kept darting over to me and then back to the road, clearly torn between wanting to avoid an accident and looking at me.

"No! I mean, uh, you can do something with Amy if you want to," he said, "but I was thinking maybe you and I could do something together tomorrow."

It was several hours before I stopped smiling.

***

My date with Rhys – date! – was set for the next day at eleven in the morning. He had suggested that I dress warmly and be prepared to spend time outside. Since it was late April, on any given day it was possible that there would be rain, so despite the appearance of sunshine that morning, I brought a jacket and wore several layers. Not exactly what I would call sexy attire, but I kind of liked the outdoorsy look.

When Rhys showed up, he proved that the outdoorsy look can look really good! He wore a charcoal Gore-Tex jacket, cut in a way that emphasized his v-shaped torso, and a black knit hat and scarf. He looked comfortable in them, like he was in his natural element. Which, when I thought about it, was probably true. He had grown up working on his father's fishing boat in Wales, so he was no stranger to the outdoors. He probably didn't have any Gore-Tex back then, but I'm sure he had other ways of staying warm and dry.

"You look beautiful," he said, giving me a shy smile.

I blushed and lowered my head. I knew he was giving me a genuine compliment, but even after all these months since my change I still had difficulty figuring out how to respond to compliments about my looks. It wasn't something that came naturally to me.

"Thanks," I said after a slight hesitation. "You look really nice, too." Oh, no, that didn't sound dumb at all.

We drove to the Oregon coast and out to a small seafood restaurant with a gorgeous view of the ocean. I had seen it before, but had never been inside.

There was a line of people waiting to get in as we arrived. Rhys calmly made his way up to the perky blonde hostess with a name tag that read Heather.

"How may I help you?" she asked, and I saw her eye Rhys appreciatively. I felt an instant dislike for her.

"Reservation for Owen," Rhys said.

"Well, we're rather backed up right now," said Heather, in a nasty flirty tone.

Hello? Did she not see Rhys was with me?

She looked down at the reservation book, and had opened her mouth to say more, but instead she quickly looked back up and had a different kind of expression on her face. Her leering smile had been replaced by a nervous grimace. She glanced at me and back at Rhys.

"This way, Mr. Owen," she said.

Heather led us through the crowded dining area into a large banquet room that could have easily held two dozen people, but was completely empty. That seemed odd given the line outside.

She sat us at a table by the window with a gorgeous ocean view. Through the glass I could faintly hear the rhythmic crashing of waves.

Our waiter – a guy, thankfully – took our drink orders and brought them back almost instantly. While we decided on our entrées, he waited in the far corner of the room, clearly torn between giving us privacy and being available when we were ready to order. Were we his only customers?

"What's going on?" I asked Rhys.

"What do you mean?"

"We're in this big room by ourselves while there's a line of people waiting to get in. The hostess got really nervous when you gave her your name, and our waiter seems to be waiting only on us."

Rhys shrugged and seemed a little embarrassed. "It's not a mystery. When I made reservations, I told them I wanted to rent the entire back room. I knew this place could get crowded on the weekend, and I wanted to make this a relaxing afternoon for you."

I took a quick sip of my drink to hide the look of shock on my face. Had he rented out the entire back half of the restaurant? I didn't know how much that cost, but I was pretty sure it was more than anyone had spent on a date for me before - unless you counted the Mercedes Eric bought for me that my dad made me give back.

I ordered the swordfish and Rhys had mahi-mahi. The food was delicious, gently touched with spices to set off the natural flavor. I liked seafood, but I rarely got to have it. Dad wasn't a big fan so we almost never went to seafood restaurants.

"How's the swordfish?" Rhys asked once I had eaten a few bites.

"Unbelievable," I said.

"I'm glad." He paused and looked around the restaurant, but the only other person besides us was the waiter hovering in the far corner of the room. "I, uh, just wanted to..." Rhys trailed off and looked away.

"Wanted to?" I prompted.

Rhys broke out of his reverie. "Nothing," he said. "It was just a dumb question, and I finally remembered the answer."

"Oh, okay," I said, not sure how else to respond to such an obvious lie. What was going on with him? He was seriously confusing me.

For dessert we had a light sorbet that was just sweet enough to taste good, and not so sweet it made my overly-sensitive taste buds want to gag. It was nice to be with someone who understood the cuisine challenges associated with being a Berserker.

After we ate, we went out to Haystack Rock – one of my favorite spots on the entire coast. I loved looking out at the huge rock formation that jutted out of the ocean like a small mountain. I had a photograph in my room that my dad had taken of me and my mom when I was three. It shows us walking on the beach holding hands while the sun peeks over the top of the rock. Something about that picture always made me feel calm and safe. It had been the one constant in my room as I went through different decorating phases.

We walked along the beach together – side by side, but not touching in any way, much to my dismay – listening to the sound of waves and the cries of the gulls. The biting wind blew a light mist off the ocean so I was glad I had bundled up.

Then Rhys asked me a question that took me completely by surprise.

"Do you like me, Madison?"

I tensed, not sure where this was going. "Of course I do," I said. "You're a great guy. What's not to like?"

"Not like that," said Rhys. He stopped walking and turned to face me, standing dizzyingly close to me, so that I had to look up to meet his eyes. "Do you like me? You know, as more than just a friend?"

Was he really so oblivious that he had to ask? I had done everything I could think of to let him know how I felt. Boys really were dumb.

"Yes," I said, gazing into his eyes. "I do."

He met my gaze for a moment then turned to look out at the ocean. "I like you, too."

I reached up and turned his face so he was looking towards me again. "Then that's a good thing," I said.

"But I shouldn't," he said. "I shouldn't like you."

"Why not?"

"Think about it." A note of bitterness crept into his voice. "I'm one hundred and seventy-eight years old. You're sixteen. I should be arrested for even thinking about you like this."

"You said yourself that physically, you were only twenty."

"It's more than just that," Rhys said. His eyes were glistening. "You're the daughter of my oldest friend. What do you think your dad would say if we told him we were together?"

The pieces of the past months were now starting to click into place. Rhys did like me. He'd just been holding back out of respect for my dad.

"I would hope he'd be happy that I found someone I truly cared about," I said. "And if he had any problem with that then he and I would have to arm wrestle to settle the argument." I hoped a little humor might ease up the tension.

A smile briefly flashed across Rhys' lips. "I've never met anyone like you before, Madison."

"Well, we can't all have Berserker dads and Binder moms," I said.

"It's not about that at all," Rhys said. "There's so much more to you than just your powers. I cut out my own heart over a century ago when I left Anwyn. I vowed I would never love again and for the first time since then, I think that I could."

As he spoke he leaned in closer to me. We were now mere inches apart, and I was definitely having trouble breathing. Did he just say that he loved me?

And then the moment I had been waiting for finally came. Rhys leaned down and oh-so-gently pressed his lips to mine. My heart began pounding and I slipped into a pre-zerk, heightening my senses, increasing my awareness.

The soft touch of his lips spread through me – a warm, blissful feeling coursing through my veins. I wrapped my arms around his neck, inhaling his distinctive scent – a smell that I couldn't possibly describe, but that somehow conjured in me images of strength and goodness.

He pulled back. Our gazes met and for a moment, like that first time, I felt as if I was looking into his soul. This time, I did not pull back or break the contact. I saw pain there, and I understood its source, but I also saw hope. Hope and love.

I leaned in and rested my head on his shoulder. "I can't tell you how long I've been waiting for this moment," I said.

Rhys chuckled. "Probably about as long as I have." He took in a deep breath and reached down to squeeze my hand.

"Are you sure you want to do this?" he asked.

I squeezed back. "I've never been more sure of anything in my life." I stood up on my tiptoes and kissed him again. I reveled in the feel of his arms wrapping around me, pulling me in close.

When we were done, Rhys reached into his pocket and pulled out a rectangular wooden box. "Here," he said. "I want you to have this."

The wooden box gleamed red in the sunlight. There were tiny

brass hinges on the long side and a matching clasp opposite.

I opened the clasp and lifted the lid. There, nestled in a satin lining was a beautifully carved wooden spoon. The handle was carved so it looked as if there were two intertwined hearts that merged into an intricately carved Celtic knot. The threads of the knot merged back into a single thread which was connected to a heart-shaped bowl at the end.

"It's beautiful," I said.

"It's a love spoon," Rhys said. "It's a tradition in my homeland for a boy to carve a spoon for the girl he is interested in. If she accepts it, then that means she would like him to court her. It's sort of a declaration of intent."

"You carved this yourself?"

Rhys shrugged as if it were no big deal. I ran my fingers over the intricate carving. It had to have taken months of work. The amount of thought and effort that had gone into this was incredible.

I threw my arms around Rhys, careful not to hurt the spoon. "Thank you. I love it!"

"Then you accept my intent to court you?"

Well, that was a no-brainer. Of course I wanted to date him. But as I was opening my mouth to reply, words that Mallika had said to me earlier made me shut it again.

"I love it, Rhys, I really do," I said, not meeting his eyes.

Rhys inhaled sharply. "Please tell me you aren't about to throw a conjunction out to start your next sentence."

"But," I said, and his head drooped. "I need to tell you something to make sure you want to be in this relationship." I didn't want to tell him this because I didn't want to give him any reasons to change his mind, but my conscience said I had to at least let him know.

"Then there's nothing to discuss," Rhys said. "If you will have me, then nothing else matters."

"What if I aged like a normal human?" I asked.

"You're a Berserker, so that's not an issue."

"I'm also a Binder," I said. "Mallika said there's the possibility that I might age normally."

With a gentleness that can only come from someone incredibly strong, Rhys pulled me into an embrace. "I will take whatever time with you I can have and count myself blessed beyond my wildest hopes."

"But what if I get old and wrinkly?"

Rhys reached down and lifted my chin. "Nothing," he said, "I repeat, nothing, will keep me away from you. I gave up love once for the Berserker cause. I will not do so again."

I reached up and pulled Rhys' head closer to me. "That is exactly what I was hoping to hear." I pulled him inward for a rather passionate kiss that I sincerely hoped would be the first of many to come.

CHAPTER 6

THE PLAY'S THE THING

At school on Monday I walked into the building holding hands with Rhys. The gossip machine kicked into high gear within milliseconds of our arrival. By the time we got to my locker, I was pretty sure the entire school knew Rhys and I were an item – finally.

Amy ran up to me and practically knocked me over giving me a giant hug. Then she let go and punched me in the arm.

"How could you not tell me?" she said.

"I'm sorry, but it just happened, and I've been a bit distracted."

Amy looked over at Rhys. "I bet you have been."

I blushed. "Oh, not like that."

"Hey, I'm not judging." She leaned in closer and whispered, "What are you going to tell Josh?"

"The truth. I'm dating Rhys and no longer available."

"He's going to be devastated," said Amy.

"I doubt it."

Amy hesitated before speaking, not meeting my eyes. "Well, would you mind if I did some consoling, should the need arise?"

"Knock yourself out," I said.

The morning had a surreal feeling to it. I recalled the first day of school this year, when I had come in looking completely different and everyone seemed to be staring at me. What was it about high school that made everyone so interested in things that were none of their business?

By the time lunch approached I was both looking forward to it and dreading it. I was looking forward to spending some time alone with Rhys – if you can count being in a cafeteria full of staring hormone-riddled teenagers as being alone – but I was also dreading my first contact with Josh. I hadn't seen him all day.

We arrived first and sat at our usual table. I felt the eyes watching me and did my best to ignore them. Rhys didn't seem to mind the attention.

"Who cares?" he said. "I was never worried about what any of them thought."

I grabbed his hand and gave it a squeeze. "That's tough talk from a man who's scared to let my dad know we're dating." We had jointly decided to let our relationship grow a bit before subjecting it to the fire of my dad's potential ire. But it couldn't hurt to tease him a bit about it.

"Hey-" But before he could finish his protest, he stiffened and looked over my shoulder.

I glanced back and saw Josh walking towards us. The half-grin on his face gave him an insolent, almost cocky expression.

"Hey, Madison," he said when he reached the table. "Can we talk for a second? You know, alone?"

I was about to tell him that anything he had to say he could tell me in front or Rhys, but Rhys let go of my hand and said, "Why don't you two talk. I'll be back in a minute." He stood up and quietly slipped out of the cafeteria.

Josh pulled up an empty chair and sat on it backwards, leaning his arms on the back rest.

"So, you two are going out now?" he asked.

"That's right," I said cautiously, unsure which direction this conversation was going to go.

"Don't think I'm giving up, Madison," he said.

"Josh, look," I said, trying for a combination of compassion and firmness. "It's over between us and has been for a long time. You need to accept that Rhys and I are together."

"I accept this as the price I have to pay for messing things up with us before." His face clouded over with a look of confusion. "I still don't know what I was thinking, but I intend to fix my mistakes and get you back. Arthur didn't give up when he saw Guinevere fall for Lancelot."

"Yeah, and look how well that turned out. They destroyed an entire kingdom."

Josh smiled and stood up. "Some things are worth fighting for."

***

The rest of the week went by in a blur of rehearsal, school, constant staring, Berserker training, and Binder lessons.

All of which – except for the staring; that was really getting on my nerves – was fine with me. I got to spend most of each day with Rhys, and I didn't have time to do much more than keep my head above water, which made the days go by quickly.

By opening night, I was feeling confident and excited. I knew my parts backwards and forwards. I was ready to show everyone what we'd been working so hard on.

Amy, on the other hand, looked positively green. Not with envy, but more like someone who just got off a giant rollercoaster and was stumbling around looking for a place to throw up.

"Why do I let you talk me into these things?" she said, as we put on our stage makeup in the girls' changing room.

"You just have opening night jitters," I said. "It's perfectly normal. You'll do fine." Looking for a way to distract her, I said, "Have you made any progress with Josh?"

Amy scowled. "No. Stupid boy only has eyes for you. He's completely blind to all my hints and suggestions."

"Well, please keep trying," I said. "Honestly, you're doing me a huge favor."

"I will. But I'm going to have to switch to tougher tactics if this keeps up."

When the curtain went up I was pleased to see Mom and Dad in the audience, as well as Mallika and Kara. For the first time in the history of our musical productions, we actually sold out opening night. Part of it was because we had a diverse cast this year and were pulling in friends from more than just the drama kids, but I was pretty certain that the real life love drama between Josh, Rhys, and myself had brought in a few people.

The play opened up well enough, with no major mess-ups or forgotten lines. When it came time for me to sing the Simple Joys of Maidenhood, I felt more alive than I could remember. I sang with all my energy, but in the back of my head, I couldn't help thinking that Guinevere was a bit of an idiot for wanting men to fight over her. I still loved the song, but these days I looked at it differently.

Actually, I felt pity for her. At that point in the play she was young and naïve, an insecure girl who simply wanted to feel loved and desired. She was too inexperienced to know the pain her actions would cause.

She learned by the end.

The song "What do the Simple Folk do" was supposed to end with Josh holding me tenderly in his arms as the curtains closed. Instead, Josh bent down and kissed me gently on the lips.

I was so shocked that I couldn't help pre-zerking, but I held off reacting as the crowd burst into applause. Once the curtains had closed though, I let Josh have it.

"You idiot!" I hissed. "What was that?"

"Sorry," he said, his grin clearly showing no remorse. "I just got caught up in the part."

I punched him in the shoulder - forgetting that I was pre-zerking.

He staggered off-balance for several steps and fell to the floor, clutching his arm.

His expression wavered from shock, to confusion, and then I saw his eyes widen with fear momentarily. He gave me a confused look and walked off without saying anything.

The prop people needed to prepare the stage for the next scene, so I stormed off the stage. I was angry about what Josh had done – wasn't it some sort of sexual assault to kiss someone without their permission? – but I was even more angry with myself for losing control. I hadn't meant to hit him very hard, but when you add in the pre-zerk...

Plus, that look on his face had me worried. I had only seen him look scared once before: right after our first kiss, when I had almost killed him. Was the haze wearing off? Could it wear off? There were so many things I didn't know.

My thoughts were interrupted by a scraping noise and a gasp from above. It was faint, even to my pre-zerking senses, so I doubted anyone else had heard it. I looked up toward the system of scaffolding and catwalks that formed a sort of metallic web overhead.

The noise came again. It was coming from stage-left, but wooden walking planks prevented me from seeing the source. I had a bit of a break before my next scene. On impulse, I walked to one of the ladders leading up and started climbing.

Using my pre-zerking reflexes, I quickly ascended the ladder and stepped onto the web of catwalks. It was dark up there, but about twenty feet away, at the edge of the stage I saw a flash of red and movement in the shadows.

Grateful for my increased balance, I ran toward the disturbance. As I approached, I had a difficult time understanding what it was that I saw. In the dim light I made out three separate images – a bucket filled with some sort of red liquid; Ginger Johnson, lying flat on her back and thrashing around; and a black monster that looked like shadow come to life and was apparently trying to eat Ginger.

I really didn't like Ginger. Even so, I didn't hesitate to act. I sped across the catwalk and pulled the creature off of her. It thrashed about, clearly upset to be taken from its prey.

The thing was jet black, a darkness so deep that it blended perfectly with the shadows. An almost skeletal head filled with sharp black teeth snapped and twisted, trying to reach me, but I held it firmly by the throat. Six legs with sharp claws flailed in a vain attempt to rake my flesh.

Ginger scrambled back, almost knocking over the bucket of red liquid – was that paint? – a look of terror in her eyes. She held a hand to her throat where red marks and bloody scratches welling showed she had been attacked. She breathed in small gasps, a look of pain accompanying each wheeze.

The creature's skin had a slimy texture, like holding a frog. As I squeezed, I felt something break, and instead of simply compressing the creature's neck, my hand squished through it like demonic play dough. Bits of the creature oozed through my fingers, leaving my hands clenched into a fist around nothing. Unfortunately, at that moment, the creature solidified again, trapping my fist within it. I threw up my arms, trying to fling the creature off me, but it held fast, keeping my hands trapped together.

Slowly, the creature wrapped its six legs around me, stretching and oozing to surround me. Its head twisted one hundred and eighty degrees on its neck so that I stood face to face with the creature, my hands still trapped together, and my body completely enveloped.

I didn't want to fully 'zerk in the middle of the school with Ginger watching, but I had a feeling it wouldn't have helped anyway. On instinct, much the same way I had fought the Bringers the first time, I tapped into my Binder powers. Instead of trying to pull free, I attempted to cast a snare.

I pushed hard, willing the tendrils to come and wrap up the creature. To my surprise, instead of entangling the creature, black tendrils burst out of it, shattering its hold on me.

The creature fell onto the catwalk. I took a staggering step back, hands still held out, casting the snare. The thick tendrils looked almost grey in comparison to the pure blackness of the monster.

Where the tendrils touched the creature, a faint acrid smoke wafted upward. It struggled against the snare, and then began convulsing. Finally it lay still, the blackness fading from it, revealing a greenish mound of nasty ripped apart monster.

A vibration of the cat-walk alerted me that we were not alone. I turned around to see Rhys running toward me in full 'zerk, Kara cradled in his arms.

He set Kara down beside me, and she bent to examine the creature. Rhys dropped the 'zerk – apparently not caring that Ginger was there – and pulled me into his arms.

"Are you all right?" he asked. "I felt you pre-zerk, but I figured you were mad about Josh kissing you." His eyes darkened. "I will have a talk with him, by the way. But when it didn't stop I figured something was wrong and texted Kara to come back-stage." He looked at the bound creature. "What is that?"

Kara shook her head, her face pale. "I think we need to get Mallika up here." She looked up at me. "But you both need to get back down to the play. I'll clean up here." She jerked her head towards Ginger. "And take care of her."

I nodded numbly, reaching out and embracing Rhys. He bent down and gently kissed me. Together we climbed back down the ladder to the stage.

Amy saw us coming down together and rolled her eyes. "You couldn't wait until the play was over?" she asked, giving me a wink.

We made it through the rest of the play without incident. I noticed Josh holding his right arm awkwardly and wondered how badly I had hurt him. Part of me felt guilty for it, but another part of me was really mad at him for kissing me like that and thought he deserved what he got.

It took me a while, but by the time Rhys sang "If Ever I Would Leave You" I had once again completely submerged into the part of Guinevere. Watching Rhys sing the words of Lancelot, I couldn't help but cry, tears cascading down my face as he sang of undying love. The end of that scene got particularly loud applause.

After the final scene, I went out to take my bow with a mixture of relief that everything had gone well – if you didn't include the monster attacking Ginger in the middle of the play – and sadness that opening night was over. The other performances would be good, but nothing was ever as exciting as opening night.

When Rhys, Josh, and myself all held hands and bowed as Mrs. Abrams had showed us, I was pleasantly surprised to get a standing ovation that seemed to last for ages. As soon as the curtains closed, Josh let go of my hand as if it were something hot, or dangerous. He didn't say anything to me, and marched straight out of the auditorium and into the main lobby where the cast could go meet family and friends.

Rhys took my hand and together we walked out into the chaos, listening to hundreds of people congratulate us on our performance. At any other time I would have reveled in the wonderful post-production euphoria, but instead I wanted to find Kara and Mallika and ask what had happened to that creature.

Fortunately, Kara found us. She pulled me in for a hug and whispered, "Don't worry, it's all taken care of."

I gave her a quick squeeze before she moved on and let others congratulate us. A few moments later my mom and dad came down the hall, a large bouquet of roses in Mom's arms. She handed them to me and gave me a hug and a kiss.

"Oh, Madison," she said. "You were wonderful! I could practically see the tears in your eyes when Rhys sang to you. You have a real gift."

"Yes, you do," said Dad, and he hugged me, too. They gushed

over my performance for a few minutes before stepping back to let others congratulate Rhys and me.

"We'll see you at home," Mom said as they left.

We spent the next half hour socializing with various friends, well-wishers, and random audience members who wanted to meet the cast before we went back into the dressing rooms to change.

Mallika and Kara met us in the lobby and we all went out to the Range Rover together. We talked on the way, but only about inconsequential things. None of us wanted to be overheard discussing what had happened on the catwalk.

In the back of the Range Rover, the dead monster lay wrapped in a blue tarp, a rancid smell wafting up from its corpse. Mallika and Kara had managed to sneak it off of the cat-walk and into the vehicle during the play.

"How did you get it here?" I asked.

Mallika smiled. "We're stronger than we look."

I blinked. "What does that even mean?"

"She means we used the binding to move the wee beastie," Kara said. "Mind over muscle, you know."

"No, actually I didn't know," I said. "I had no idea you could use a binding to move objects."

"I'm more interested in what it is," said Rhys. He turned the ignition and started the Range Rover. "I've never seen anything like it before."

Mallika and Kara both looked at each other.

"The 'what' isn't much of a problem," Mallika finally said. "The bigger questions are 'how' and 'who'."

Rhys fixed Mallika with a fierce stare. "I've never questioned you before about Binder secrets," he said. "You know I trust you and respect your loyalties, but we can't let Binder politics to get in the way of our work here. Madison could have died up there, and an innocent girl – well, sort of innocent – could have been killed."

I could hardly believe what I was hearing. Everyone had warned me there were secrets and political games between the Binders and Berserkers, but this was the first time I had been directly affected by it.

"Believe me," said Mallika, "no one is more shocked about what happened than I am." She put a hand on Rhys' shoulder. "Do not worry, we will tell you all, as we would have even without your rebuke. I do not forget that we are on the same side, Rhys."

Rhys squeezed Mallika's hand. "Thank-you."

"The creature Madison killed is called an Azark," Mallika said. "It has the unique ability of being invisible to humans, and Berserkers as well."

"But I saw-" I began.

"You are a special case," said Mallika, holding up a hand to cut me off, "and ordinary rules do not seem to apply to you, my dear. Other than you, no Berserker or human can see an Azark while it is living. The only ones who can see a living Azark, are Binders."

"But why?" I asked.

"Because Azarks have a special link to the Binders," said Mallika. "They are our weapons, our assassins."

It took me a minute to process what Mallika was saying. "That creature was summoned by a Binder?" I asked.

Mallika nodded. "Which means that one of the Binders wants you dead."

CHAPTER 7

FIGMENT OF MY IMAGINATION

Who would want her dead?" demanded Rhys.

Mallika looked around at the quickly emptying parking lot. "Perhaps it would be prudent to begin our journey home?"

Rhys put the Range Rover in drive and stomped on the gas, shooting us out of the parking lot at a ridiculously fast speed. The way he was driving you might think he was the one trying to kill me.

"To answer your question," Mallika said. "I do not know who would want her dead, but I would speculate that her unique gift of being both a Binder and a Berserker has made someone feel threatened. This person sent an Azark to kill her, unaware that she would be uniquely qualified to defeat it."

"Why haven't I ever heard of an Azark before?" asked Rhys. He made a sharp right turn, sending all of us scrambling for something to hold on to. I grabbed the handle over the window and just held on for the ride.

"Because they are a Binder secret," Mallika said. "I know you do not trust the Binder Conclave, but you must understand that there are reasons for the secrets we keep."

"And what's your reason for concealing your ability to summon invisible assassins?" Rhys asked, a hint of sarcasm in his voice.

"Because they are intended to kill Berserkers and they work best when they can attack unawares."

"What?" I shouted. I couldn't keep quiet any longer. "Why would you want to kill a Berserker? You're on the same side."

I expected Rhys to join in with some particularly savage righteous indignation. Instead, when he spoke, it was practically in a whisper.

"They have reason, Madison. There are times when it is required."

I remembered what they had told me about Berserkers going feral. They had even told me about the oaths they took to kill each other should that happen.

"A Binder is allowed to summon an Azark in only two cases," Mallika said. "One is when the Berserker has gone feral and becomes a danger to those around him."

"And the other?"

Kara answered. "The other is when a Berserker has been captured and is being taken to break a binding. When that happens, it is permitted to summon an Azark to kill a Berserker before he reaches the seal and his life's blood can be used to free a Havoc."

"Well, I didn't see either of those happening tonight," I said.

"Sadly, you are right," said Mallika. "And that means we have a traitor in our midst."

Traitor. The word hung heavy in the air, a palpable weight to it.

"Kara and I must report this to the Conclave as quickly as possible."

We drove in silence for a few minutes before Rhys spoke. "Do you think it's really a good idea to discuss what happened with the Binder Conclave?" he asked. "Given the fact that the traitor is a Binder?"

"That is exactly why we need to bring it to the Conclave," Mallika said.

I could literally feel the tension escalating between them, so I decided to move the topic to something we could all be unified against.

"What happened with Ginger?" I asked. "Did you find out what she was doing up there in the first place?"

"Well, that's where the Azark did you a bit of a favor," said Kara. "Saved you some serious embarrassment."

"What do you mean?"

"Did you ever read the book Carrie, where they dumped a bucket of pig blood on that girl during Prom? Well, she was planning her own improvised version of that scene with a bucket of red paint. Next thing she knew some invisible monster had jumped on her, and then you showed up."

"Did you put a haze on her?" I asked.

"No."

"What? But she saw Rhys 'zerk, saw me kill the Azark. What if she tells someone?"

"We've spoken with her," said Mallika, "and explained the necessity of keeping this secret. I don't think she'll be a problem."

"But why?" I asked. "Wouldn't it just be safer to wipe her memory?"

"I sometimes forget how new you are to all this," Mallika said. "A haze doesn't erase the memory, it just renders it inaccessible. This poor girl was quite traumatized and needs time to process what happened to her. If we put a haze on her now, she won't consciously remember what happened, and will be unable to come to grips with what she experienced. Without time to process this traumatic experience she will suffer from nightmares and anxieties for years to come. At times we deem that a necessary price for our secrecy, but in this case it seemed unlikely she would tell anyone what happened tonight."

Were they talking about the same Ginger I knew? The Ginger I knew would break a promise in a heartbeat if it meant causing me pain or embarrassment.

"I'm with Madison on this," said Rhys. "Ginger would remove her own liver if it meant causing Madison pain."

"Don't worry," said Kara. "We'll keep an eye on her and take necessary measures if the need arises."

I doubted there was much *if* to it - it seemed more like *when* to me - but it was obvious they had already made up their minds. They certainly wouldn't be the only ones keeping an eye on Ginger.

The Range Rover turned into my driveway, and I said an awkward goodbye to everyone. I really could have used a few hours wrapped in Rhys' comforting embrace, but since no one knew about the two of us yet – that was going to need to change really soon – there was no way that was going to happen tonight.

Once I got inside, I told Dad what had happened. I knew he would freak out and get all uberprotective on me, but I was pretty sure Mallika or Rhys would have told him tomorrow anyway, and I wanted to downplay the seriousness of it so I wouldn't be confined to my room for the rest of eternity.

For my own safety, of course.

Unfortunately, no matter how I tried to spin it, the mere mention of the possibility of a Binder traitor triggered Dad's knee-jerk reflexes. He immediately went into his office and began making phone calls.

Too emotionally drained to argue with him, I changed into my pajamas and crawled into bed. I tried to sleep, but even as exhausted as I was, I ended up tossing and turning.

After an hour of sleepless frustration, I got out of bed and opened my window. The moon shone through the branches of the trees, casting strange shadows and lighting the night. Ordinarily, I loved looking out at our yard at night. The night noises and the feel of a cool breeze on my face always gave me a peaceful feeling. But tonight, it took on a sinister tone as I thought about the Azark that had been sent to kill me.

At the edge of our yard, I caught sight of movement near the bushes. Immediately, I pre-zerked and searched the yard with my enhanced vision.

Seconds later, I felt a 'zerking from nearby. Right where I had seen movement.

Rhys stepped out of the shadows, his varé drawn and his body crouched into a defensive posture.

I changed to a full 'zerk long enough to jump out the window, landing on my feet and using one arm for balance. I then dropped the 'zerk and approached Rhys.

"What are you doing here?" I asked.

Rhys switched off his 'zerk. He looked sheepish. "Don't be mad," he said, "but given what happened tonight, I thought it might be a good idea if I stood guard. Just in case."

I wrapped my arms around Rhys' broad chest, laying my head on his shoulder. "That's very sweet," I said. "Except that if another Azark comes tonight, since you can't see it, I'm likely to have to come rescue you."

"The Azark depends heavily on the element of surprise. Now that I know what it is and what it can do, I can fight it. I have a few tricks up my sleeve that should work nicely."

I gave Rhys a squeeze and said nothing. I really didn't want to talk Azark killing tactics and strategies. I preferred to stay silent and enjoy the feel of being in his arms.

***

Saturday morning existed for me in theory only. Intellectually, I knew that Saturday morning followed Friday night, but since I managed to sleep right through it, I had no conscious recollection of it. I had stayed up with Rhys for more than an hour before he insisted I go to bed so he could properly guard me. By that time I was exhausted enough that I didn't argue.

My mom woke me up just after noon so I could eat and get ready to do the first of two performances today – one at two and one at six.

Rhys picked me up at one and we drove to the school to get into makeup and costume. On the way he told me that Kara had cut the Azark into seven pieces and buried each of them in a different location.

When I asked him why, he simply said, "You can never take too many precautions. We want to make sure this thing stays dead."

Our first performance of the day went off with only a few hitches. A couple of people missed their cues and the techs in the sound booth accidentally started the music to "What Do The Simple Folk Do" when there were still a dozen lines of dialogue to go before the song.

Mallika and Kara were there, but neither of them sat in the audience to watch the play. Instead they prowled around the hallways and corridors looking for anything unusual. We all hoped the Azark attack was a one-time thing, but no one wanted to take any chances.

Josh kept his distance from me when we were not on stage together. I hadn't really spoken to him since he had kissed me and I had – justifiably – punched him in the arm. Hard. Okay, maybe a bit too hard. I was beginning to wonder if that punch hadn't somehow triggered his memory of our first kiss. I would have to keep an eye on him just in case.

It didn't take Amy long to notice that Josh wasn't hanging around me. She immediately began a full-out assault, ready to take the opportunity as it presented itself. She found excuses to spend time with him when neither of them were on stage and began dropping hints about Prom. After all, it was only a couple of weeks away.

All of which was fine with me. It was too stressful trying to manage two guys at once. I was glad I was in a committed relationship without any complications - except for the not telling my dad or other Berserkers and Binders part.

Sigh.

Between performances, Mrs. Abrams ordered pizza and the cast ate together. Amy sat by Josh – no surprise there – and grinned at me when he stood up to get her another slice of pizza. He came back and sat with his arm wrapped around the back of her chair, so close she was practically in his lap. How did she do that to guys? I had thought she was like Machiavelli, with schemes and plans, but Josh was reacting too quickly for this to be a scheme. Schemes took time. This was more like Houdini pulling off one impossible escape after another. Unbelievable.

Rhys saw where I was looking. "Does it bother you?" he asked.

"Not in the slightest," I said. "I've got the man I want." I scooted closer to him and leaned my head on his shoulder, basking in his warmth. It was amazing that hard muscle could be so comfortable to lean against. He took my hand in his and together we sat in comfortable silence, simply enjoying each other's presence.

Our third and final performance was the best of all. We got the music issue resolved and by now everyone had gotten their initial jitters out. The performance was practically flawless.

I was deeply in character and enjoying the performance until it came time for me to sing "I Loved You Once In Silence". While singing this heart-wrenching song to Rhys, I happened to glance out over the audience. There, standing in the back, I saw a familiar face with blond spiky hair and high cheekbones.

Eric.

My pulse quickened in surprise and my senses sharpened as I pre-zerked out of sheer shock. What was he doing back? To my credit, I did manage to hold my note and remember the lyrics. Rhys, feeling me pre-zerk, got a panicked look on his face. He looked around for some sort of danger – another Azark or a Bringer.

When I reached out and took his hand, I gave him a few gentle squeezes and just slightly shook my head. He seemed to understand my message and visibly relaxed, once again submerging himself in the part of Lancelot.

By the time the choreography gave me the opportunity to look back out at the audience, Eric was gone. When the song ended, and I had the opportunity for a better look, he was nowhere to be seen.

The rest of the play went off without a hitch – it was our best overall performance. All our hard work and practice had paid off. When the final scene ended, we got a standing ovation.

I hadn't seen Eric again, and by the time we took our final bows I began to wonder if I had simply imagined him.

Before we went out to greet the audience, Rhys pulled me aside.

"What happened?" he asked. "What triggered your pre-zerk?"

"It was nothing. I just thought I saw Eric and it startled me."

Rhys smiled and shook his head.

"I should have known this would happen," he said. "I bet Scottie called the other Berserkers and told them you were in danger. They've come back to protect you."

"I don't need protection," I said, my old irritation at being under constant surveillance resurfacing.

Rhys raised an eyebrow.

His look made me deflate a bit. "Okay, at least not constant protection. Between you and me, I think I'm pretty safe."

When we went out to meet the audience, I fully expected to see Eric, his impish grin in full force. But to my surprise, he wasn't there. Maybe Rhys was wrong about my dad calling the other Berserkers, and I had just seen someone who looked like Eric.

An awful lot like him.

When Rhys dropped me off that night, we snuck in a few kisses before we went inside. We both still agreed that we weren't ready to let my dad know about us yet, so any physical affection had to be taken in small bits when we found a quiet moment alone.

After far-too-few kisses for my liking, Rhys left and I walked into the house. Dad was watching TV in the living room, so I checked with him to see if he had heard anything about the Berserkers coming back.

"No," he said. "Last I heard they were following up some heat anomalies in Indiana."

"Who did you talk to?"

"Eric."

"Did he say anything about coming back or passing through?"

Dad shook his head. "No, nothing like that. Why?"

Well, so much for that theory. I must have just seen someone who looked like him.

"Nothing. I just thought they might be coming back soon."

Dad gave me a sympathetic look. "Were you hoping he'd come back in time to see your performance? I'm sure he would have come if he could have."

"No, it's fine. I wasn't expecting him to come. I just thought I saw him earlier. No big deal."

"Really?" Dad sat up a little straighter. "Where?"

"At the play. But it was dark, and I only caught a glimpse of him in the audience. When I got a chance to look again, he was gone. I must have just seen someone who looked like him, no big deal."

I gave Dad a kiss and headed upstairs. I walked up the stairs feeling strangely disappointed. It was ridiculous, really. While it would have been great for Eric to see the play, he had more important things to be doing. Saving-the-world kinds of things. Watching my play really isn't that important when compared to that.

But the truth was I did miss Eric. Well, I did and I didn't. I did miss his sense of humor and the way he managed to make tense situations light. There was never a dull moment when Eric was around. But I also was pretty sure things wouldn't be the way they were between Rhys and me if Eric had stayed around. And I really liked the direction our relationship was going – a lot.

When I got to my room, I opened the door and flipped on the lights. I dumped my bags on the floor and stretched. Now that the post-play high had worn off, I felt exhausted. What I really needed was a good night of sleep.

It was the note that caught my eyes first. The white of the paper stood out on my dark pillowcase. In two strides I was across the room. There on my pillow was a piece of paper and two dozen roses scattered across my bed. On the note was a written a single sentence: "You have a gift."

I quickly glanced around the room, searching for other objects that looked out of place. Nothing else appeared to be disturbed. I walked to the window and saw that it was unlocked.

Had I left it unlocked, or was this the route my anonymous note-leaver had used to exit my room? I didn't generally leave my windows unlocked, but I also couldn't specifically remember locking it in the last few days.

I examined the handwriting on the note. While I was by no means an expert at handwriting, the note did look like it was written by a guy. The writing was very clear and legible – not typical guy handwriting characteristics, but it was also not filled with any frilly touches either.

I read it again. Given everything that had happened tonight, there was only one person this note could be from. I didn't have any definitive proof, but I was certain Eric had come to see the play.

CHAPTER 8

WHAT I DID ON MY SPRING BREAK

I didn't tell anyone about the note or the roses – not even Rhys. First off, I technically didn't have proof that Eric was responsible. Yes, I thought I had seen him. Yes, it certainly seemed like something he would do. And yes, I was almost certain it was him. But I didn't actually *know*.

Second, if it was Eric, I was pretty sure he wasn't supposed to be here. He had been assigned to look for Osadyn with the other Berserkers. The last thing I wanted was to get him in trouble for sneaking away to see my play.

And third, I had the feeling that Eric didn't want me to tell anyone. Not just because the other Berserkers and Binders would be upset he wasn't taking his assignment seriously. Something about the way he did this felt private, intimate almost. If he had wanted an audience he would have picked a more public place, or done something visible to everyone – like renting the Goodyear Blimp and flying it over the school.

My fourth, and last, reason was probably my most compelling one – I honestly wasn't sure how Rhys would react. Things had progressed so well between us with Eric gone, I didn't want anything to mess that up.

Sunday morning was quiet and leisurely. The play was over, and Monday would be the beginning of Spring Break. I would have the week to relax, sleep in, and just be a typical teenager. Well, except for my training lessons, but those were with Rhys, so no problem there.

That idyllic feeling lasted all of about two hours. The phone rang and Dad answered it. It was Mallika, telling him my lessons were canceled for the week.

"Why?" I asked once he had hung up.

"Something is going on down in Mexico, where Thuanar is bound. Rhys just got a report of some suspicious activity down there. He and Kara are going down to check it out."

Rhys was going to go down to Mexico? Without me? There was no way I was going to let *that* happen without a fight.

"I want to go," I said.

I had just started developing my argument on why I should go, when Dad completely shocked me.

"I think you should go," he said.

I hadn't been expecting that. I was all prepared for another classic father-daughter battle – butting heads and making overly-dramatic threats.

"Really?"

Dad took in a deep breath and let it out. "Yeah. I think you should go."

I didn't trust this at all. This was some sort of trap. My dad would never willingly let me put myself in danger. "What, no arguments about how dangerous it is and how I should stay here where it's safe?"

With a sad half-smile Dad reached out and squeezed my hand. "Not anymore," he said. "You've proven your capabilities time after time. You're as much a Berserker as I ever was and fully understand the risks. I can't keep holding you back."

I was struck by how much my life had changed in less than a year. My dad was finally coming to trust me and see me as an equal – a true Berserker and not just a sixteen-year-old girl who needed protecting. This trip was a huge milestone in our relationship, one that I would remember as a turning point in my life.

I gave him a hug. "Thanks Dad, that means a lot to me."

He squeezed me back. "Well, I better start booking our tickets if we are going to fly out tomorrow."

"We? Wait, you're coming too?"

"Of course, you didn't think I was going to let you go down to Mexico without me?"

Or maybe things hadn't changed that much.

***

Once Rhys' found out my dad was in favor of me going to Mexico, he didn't argue with me or even try to convince me to stay.

That was almost as surprising as my dad agreeing in the first place. Just when I think I have things figured out people change, and I have to start all over again.

The flight to Mexico was pretty uneventful. Rhys filled me in on all the details on the way down. When a Havoc is bound it is tied to a specific location. In order for someone to free the Havoc, the life blood of a Berserker must be spilled on the seal marking the binding location. That means they have to sacrifice a *living* Berserker on the spot to free the Havoc. To prevent that from happening, the Binder Council keeps watch on all the bound Havocs. Ideally they have Binders there to send out Azarks that would kill a Berserker before his blood could be used to break the seal. The blood of a dead Berserker has no effect.

But the reality is that watching the binding locations is a boring and tedious job. Unless there is some warning of a Berserker missing or in danger, they hire trusted people to keep watch and be on the lookout for anyone who appears to be too interested in the seals.

A few days ago, the person watching Thuinar's seal down in Puebla, Mexico had reported a couple of suspicious people who appeared to be examining Thuinar's binding location. Since they were not a Binder or a Berserker, they wouldn't be able to see the seal or the Havoc, but they were measuring and making marks that appeared to be too close to the seal for it to be a coincidence.

"It's probably nothing," said Rhys, from his seat next to me. "We've had false alarms before. After a few months of watching, the people monitoring the seals start seeing sinister intentions in innocent people and activities. I would have ignored this one, but the Binder Council specifically asked us to go check it out."

"What makes them think this is an actual threat?" I asked.

"I don't know," said Rhys. "They told me we would get more information when we got there."

***

We arrived mid-evening and took a taxi from the airport to the hotel. The air was humid and warm, full of unfamiliar smells – some good, some not so much.

Our taxi driver tore through the streets like Dale Earnhardt on meth. He weaved in and out of traffic, forcing his way into tiny openings, clearly convinced that other drivers would let him in rather than risk a wreck. Every turn was like a game of chicken. The concept of lanes appeared to have been abandoned all together, with cars squeezing in wherever they could find room. Once, he even pulled partway onto the sidewalk to get around another car.

When I had driven onto the sidewalk, the examiner failed me on my driver's test. Here it seemed to be the norm. The pedestrians appeared to be completely used to it and simply walked around the car. Clearly the driving rules were a little looser down here.

With the protection I had from my Berserker powers I probably shouldn't have been nervous, but that didn't stop me from letting out a huge thank-goodness-I'm-still-alive-don't-ever-make-me-do-that-again sigh when we pulled up to the hotel.

We checked in and put our bags in the rooms. Kara and I shared a room, and Rhys and my Dad shared another. We could have easily afforded our own rooms, but both Dad and Rhys insisted sharing rooms was safer.

I wasn't sure exactly what they were afraid of – we were by far the most dangerous beings around – but I didn't put up a fight.

We had dinner in the hotel restaurant. It was delicious, with only a few items being overwhelming to my enhanced taste. We didn't have any way to meet up with our contact down here until tomorrow morning, so after some wheedling from Kara and myself, we convinced Rhys and Dad to explore the city a bit.

Our hotel was in a busy area with plenty to explore within walking distance. We wandered the streets taking in the sights and sounds of the city. My Spanish was very limited, so I could only guess at the meaning of the words on signs. Rhys, however, was perfectly at ease and as far as I could tell, completely fluent in Spanish.

"It's another one of the perks of a long life," he said when I questioned him about it.

"Kind of like becoming an accomplished actor and memorizing all of Camelot?" I asked.

"Something like that."

I wanted to hold his hand while we walked, but that wasn't going to happen with my dad chaperoning us. Instead we walked awkwardly by each other, wanting to be together, but having to pretend we didn't.

Until Kara came to the rescue.

"Scottie, I'm not feeling very well," she said. "I think I need to go back to the hotel. Would you walk me back?" She gave me a surreptitious wink, and I tried to hide my grin.

"Maybe we should all call it a night," my Dad said. "We do want to be rested for tomorrow."

"I'm not tired," I said, perhaps a bit too quickly. Dad looked at me suspiciously.

"Ah Scottie, don't make them suffer because of me," said Kara. "Let the wee ones have some fun. Rhys knows the language, and I'm sure he would be more than happy to show Madison around." As she spoke, her Scottish accent grew even thicker. I wondered if that was deliberate.

Deliberate or not, it seemed to do the trick. When dad answered, I could hear a hint of his own accent coming to the surface.

"Rhys, if you don't mind?"

Rhys played it very cool, but I could see through his act. He wanted to be alone with me as much as I wanted to be with him. Hopefully, my dad couldn't tell.

"Sure, Scottie. I'd be more than happy to. That is, if Madison feels up for it?"

This time I made sure to not appear overly-eager. I tried to look thoughtful, as if weighing the pros and cons of staying with Rhys or going back to the hotel.

"Sure, why not?" I said. "It's not every day I come to Mexico."

That seemed to satisfy Dad. He and Kara headed back to the hotel, leaving Rhys and I alone. Well, surrounded by thousands of people walking through the streets, but we were anonymous and didn't have to hide our relationship from those people.

I grabbed Rhys' hand. "Come on, wee one," I said. "Let's explore."

Rhys rolled his eyes. "Wee ones, indeed. I was..." he trailed off and looked away, his cheeks flushing.

"What?" I asked.

"Never mind."

But I was pretty sure I knew what the problem was. He was still self-conscious about being so much older than me. I guess I couldn't blame him. In the majority of cases when I saw a couple with a multi-decade age difference, one of them was old, wrinkly, and wealthy while the other was young, beautiful and very interested in money. That wasn't the case with us. We were physically only a few years apart, and since I was a Berserker with a trust fund, I would have just as much money as Rhys did.

"Don't be ridiculous," I said, and pulled him down the street.

***

We spent the next hour wandering the streets and taking in the sights. It felt wonderful to just walk together holding hands without having to worry about who might see us and what anyone else might think. We were free to be ourselves.

As we walked, I gazed at the buildings and how different the architecture was here. Everything seemed elaborate and ornate with all sorts of designs and patterns carved into the buildings. Some of the buildings were pretty old and run down, but they had a feel of uniqueness to them – an individuality. It gave everything an almost hand-made feel. It was very different from the clean lines and modern look of office buildings and skyscrapers I was used to seeing in the US.

We discovered a section of town where there was a large flea market and we browsed through the selection of crafts, knockoffs, and trinkets as we wandered up and down the aisles of booths. I bought Amy a brightly colored rag doll wearing traditional Mexican clothing. We always brought home souvenirs for each other whenever we traveled someplace new.

Rhys and I were having such a good time that, without realizing it, we wandered past the flea market and into a creepy part of town. The buildings were rundown and trash littered the streets. Small groups of scary-looking guys huddled together, glaring at us as we walked.

One group did more than just glare. Four guys crossed the street and blocked our way. My initial reaction was to be scared – old habits die hard. Then I remembered that there was nothing these guys could do to hurt us... and a lot we could do to hurt them.

Rhys held out his hands in a non-threatening gesture and said something in Spanish. I guessed it was something to the effect of, "Hey guys, we don't want any trouble."

The men laughed, but not in any kind of good-natured isn't-this-amusing kind of way. It was the laugh of predators who plan on playing with their prey.

All of them were older than me, likely in their mid to late twenties. One guy had on jeans, a cowboy hat, boots, and a plaid button up shirt. He seemed to be the leader.

He walked around us very slowly, looking us up and down – especially me. He gave me a leering grin. I returned his leer with a nasty glare, but that just seemed to excite him. Gross!

The cowboy said something to Rhys in Spanish that caused Rhys to tighten his jaw and clench his fists.

"What's he saying?" I asked. Knowing book Spanish, and understanding a native speaker are two very different things.

"You don't want to know," Rhys responded. He didn't take his eyes off the cowboy.

He was probably right.

"Fine," I said. "Let's just get out of here." I grabbed Rhys' arm and pulled him back the way we came.

That didn't work so well. Two of the others stepped into our path, blocking the way. We were surrounded.

"I don't see a way out of this without a fight," said Rhys.

"Well, then let's get it over with," I said. "But let me do it."

Rhys gave me an exasperated look. "You can't seriously think I am going to let you fight these guys on your own?"

"Can you prezerk and fight these guys without glowing?" I asked.

"No, but-"

"No buts about it, Rhys. I'm the logical choice here. I appreciate the attempt at chivalry, but you aren't Lancelot and I'm not Guinevere. I don't need protection, and I can get us out of here with the least attention. Besides, I'm going to enjoy wiping that smirk off the cowboy's face."

Rhys let out an exasperated sigh. "All right. I hate it when you make sense."

I reached out and gave his hand a squeeze. "Thanks!" Did I really just thank my boyfriend for letting me beat up a bunch of guys who are accosting us in a bad part of Mexico? Wow, my life is really odd.

I took a moment and turned on my prezerk. I walked up to the cowboy guy and gave him a smile. I reached out a hand and straightened his collar. He narrowed his eyes, and grabbed my wrist - exactly what I wanted.

With almost no effort at all, I gripped his wrist with my free hand and spun around, twisting his arm behind him into a hammerlock that Rhys had taught me in one of our training sessions. It was an easy – and painful – way to control someone.

The cowboy gasped, and let out a string of what I assume was Spanish profanity. I hadn't learned *those* words.

One of his friends ran towards me, and I kicked him in the chest, sending him flying backwards and into a wall. He slid to the ground, dazed. One of the remaining two guys saw the grin on my face and ran as fast as he could in the opposite direction. He was the only smart one in the group. I let him go.

The last guy had an overly long mustache that he had twirled into points. It was a serious bad-guy mustache – like Snidely Wiplash from the old Dudley Do-Right cartoons my dad made me watch as a kid. He pulled out a gun and cocked his head to the side, letting me know he would shoot me if I didn't let go of his friend.

I contemplated throwing the cowboy guy at him, and hopefully knocking them both unconscious, but I figured there was a pretty good chance that Snidely might accidentally fire his gun. I was bulletproof, but cowboy guy was not. The whole point of my dealing with this was to keep it low-key, and a gunshot wound for anyone – even these creeps – would not be low-key.

Snidely clearly felt he had the upper hand. I played along with him and let the cowboy guy go so he would be out of the line of fire. Once I loosened my grip, cowboy guy yanked himself free as if he had simply been biding his time, rather than my helpless prisoner.

Apparently the male ego can be translated into any language.

He stood by Snidely, his arms folded, doing his best to look tough.

"Are you done playing around?" Rhys asked me.

"Give me a sec," I said. "I'm trying to not get any of them shot."

In one fluid motion, I reached forward, grabbed the gun in Snidely's hand and twisted. Without stopping, I pulled the gun from his grip, and ended with the gun pointed at him.

He had hardly had time to blink.

The sudden reversal of our situations was too much for cowboy guy and he turned around and ran, leaving Snidely at gunpoint.

I made a show of holding the gun tightly with both hands and placing the barrel directly in the center of Snidely's forehead. The blood drained from his face, his eyes began to bulge, and his lower lip trembled.

When I saw wetness spreading down the front of his pants, I decided he'd had enough. I hadn't meant to make him pee himself.

I lowered the gun and took a step back.

"Tell him to get his friend and get out of here before I change my mind," I said to Rhys. It was a total bluff, but Snidely didn't know that.

Rhys translated and Snidely grabbed his friend that I had knocked into the wall. Within moments, they were both gone and out of sight.

I held up the gun. "What do I do with this?"

"Wipe it down and trash it."

I removed the bullets and then used my pre-zerk strength to bend the gun barrel in half. I used my shirt to wipe the gun clean of finger prints and tossed it behind some crates.

Mission accomplished, I grabbed Rhys' hand. "Let's get back to the hotel."

***

We didn't tell my dad about the attackers. We hadn't been in any real danger, and it would virtually guarantee that he would not let us out of his sight for the rest of the trip. What he didn't know wouldn't hurt him.

I was pretty exhausted by the time I got back to the hotel. Kara was still awake, and she winked at me as I walked into the room.

"Don't bother thanking me," she said. "We both know you owe me."

I blushed and sat down on the edge of the bed. "I really appreciate it," I said. "It was nice to be alone with Rhys again."

"I know," said Kara. She shrugged. "I figured one of us ought to be with the man she loves."

My heart sank. I still felt awful about what happened between her and Aata. Talk about a no-win situation.

"Have you heard from him?" I asked.

Kara nodded. "Just a few texts here and there."

I hesitated, not quite brave enough to ask what I wanted to.

Kara spared me the awkwardness and answered my unasked question.

"We're no longer together. It's over."

"Oh."

"It's ok," Kara said, forcing a smile. "It really is."

I crossed my arms and gave her a flat stare. That was a complete lie and we both knew it.

"What do you want me to say?" Kara asked. "That I miss him every minute we're apart? That I think about him constantly and want nothing more than to have him hold me in his arms?" She looked up, futilely trying to blink back tears. "Of course I do. But I've come to terms with the fact that we will never be together again." Kara paused and wiped her eyes. "Sometimes I lie awake at night thinking about what I could have done differently. If I hadn't released the snare he would have died, and I would be dealing with his death instead. At least this way he's alive and there's still hope."

I had no words to respond to that. I felt horrible. I hadn't meant to force her into a painful confession of love for Aata. Feeling helpless, I reached out and hugged her as hard as I could.

***

The next morning we had breakfast at the hotel and walked to our prearranged meeting place a few blocks away. The day was beautiful – sunny and cloudless. It was too early to be really hot, but that was almost certain to change as the day progressed.

We found our contact sitting on a bench in an out-of-the-way park. If we hadn't been looking for it, we would have walked right past the entrance without even knowing it was there.

Our contact stood as soon as she saw us, clearly recognizing who we were. I guess we did kind of standout down here.

"My name is Araceli," she said. The first thing I noticed was her height. I towered over her. I wasn't exactly the tallest person in the world, but Araceli was really short. Olympic gymnast short. She had dark hair, a kind face, and a beautiful smile. She sure didn't look very dangerous.

We spent the next few minutes exchanging introductions. When I told her my name, Araceli gave me a curious look, and I wondered what she might have heard about me.

"Let me take you to the binding place, and I will tell you what has been happening."

We followed Araceli through the city, twisting and turning through narrow streets. The buildings in this part of town were so close together that it felt like walking through a maze, or a dense forest where you can't see very far or identify any landmarks to give you a point of reference.

After a while I gave up any hope of keeping my bearings and simply followed Araceli blindly. I was relieved when we finally emerged from the maze into an open area. Directly in front of us was a large, extremely ornate building surrounded by a wrought iron fence with what looked like statues of angels sitting on top. It was too large and ornate to be anything other than a cathedral. The building took up the entire block and had two large towers on either side topped with crucifixes. Definitely a cathedral.

Araceli led us through the gate and into the cathedral's courtyard. It was still relatively early in the morning, so the courtyard was not too crowded with tourists. The space was wide and flat with a few lamp posts dotting the grounds.

She strode across the courtyard and stopped in front of what looked to be a circular gold plaque in the middle of the ground. In the center of the circle was a blood-red hand print like a twisted version of those stars on the Hollywood Walk of Fame.

I bent to examine it, but as I did, I caught movement in my peripheral vision. Startled, I fell back as a creature the size of a school bus charged us.

"Look out!" I yelled. Instinctively, I rolled sideways to avoid the charging monster. It wasn't until I had jumped to my feet and caught a better look at the creature that I realized I had most likely overreacted.

The insubstantial creature reared back on its hind legs and let out a tremendous roar. Or at least, that's what I thought it was doing. Not a single sound came from it.

This must be the Havoc we had come to see: Thuanar.

They had told me the Havocs were out of phase with our world and insubstantial, but I didn't understand what that actually meant until I finally saw him.

Thuanar looked like he had stepped out of an old photograph. He was completely drained of color and his outline was slightly blurry. While Osadyn had been built like an elephant with a long neck, Thuanar's body was long and sinuous. He appeared more reptilian than Osadyn had. Spaced throughout the long body three sets of legs protruded, each ending with long talons. Two parallel rows of wicked-looking spikes ran completely down the creature's back. He looked very much like a Chinese dragon except for the face. The face was flat and squished looking, almost monkey-like.

Araceli grabbed my arm and pulled me several steps back.

"What are you doing?" She hissed in my ear.

Several people walking near us gave me strange looks, but quickly moved on. I could only imagine what I must have looked like to them – yelling and then rolling on the ground for seemingly no reason.

Now I just felt kind of dumb.

"Sorry," I said. "I just wasn't expecting that." I gestured vaguely at Thuanar. Then I realized that neither Araceli nor my dad could see Thuanar or the seal, and that my explanation was completely unenlightening.

Kara started to snicker, and I gave her my best glare. I didn't really mean it and couldn't keep it up for very long. Within a few seconds we were both laughing.

Dad just rolled his eyes. "Can we get back to the matter at hand?" he asked.

"Thank-you," said Araceli. She looked around the grounds, checking to be sure we would not be overheard.

"About a week ago, I noticed two men acting oddly. Most of the tourists are focused on the cathedral and look up or out. These two were focused on the ground, looking down. They had a stick with a wheel on it and were rolling it across the courtyard.

"At first I didn't pay too much attention to it, but I noticed them making chalk marks on the ground."

She pointed to a series of lines on the ground just a few feet away from the seal.

"I realized that the stick with a wheel on it was a measurement device and they were marking the location of the seal. Obviously I can't see it myself, but I was shown where it is by a Binder."

I tried to listen to Araceli's explanation, but I couldn't stop looking at Thuanar. As I observed him, he grew more and more agitated. He began thrashing about, whipping his long tail through the air and silently roaring. There was something about the way he moved that didn't seem right.

Because he had been bound, I knew that Thuanar couldn't hurt me, and I took a step closer. I could hear Araceli talking, but I was so focused on Thuanar that her words were just a droning background noise.

After three more steps I was directly in front of him. His thrashing slowed down and he lowered his front half back to the ground. His enormous head was almost as tall as I was. His slit pupils were bigger than my hands and looking straight at me. This was no mindless monster – I could see intelligence behind those eyes.

I reached out my hand and touched the Havoc.

Pain flowed through me, bright and sharp. I felt the hairs on my arms stand up, responding to a primeval force that I didn't even have a name for.

In an instant the world around me faded until it was washed out and drained of color. Vivid pictures flooded my mind moving faster and faster until they blurred together...

A tall man with bright red hair and full beard stood in a palace. I couldn't hear a word he said, but he was clearly agitated. He wore a single metal glove on his left hand – I had the feeling this predated Michael Jackson – and was repeatedly bashing it onto a table in frustration. Chips of wood flew out with each hit and the table looked almost ready to crack in half.

The scene changed and a muscular man sat on top of an enormous throne. His long hair hung down, obscuring half of his face. His single visible eye was fierce and I had the feeling that it missed very few things. On his shoulders sat two black birds.

One of the birds faced me and let out a squawk so loud that it echoed through the room, painfully ringing in my ears. The bird turned back to the man on the throne and put its beak to his head, seeming to whisper to him.

The man's one eye searched the room, finally stopping on me. This time I knew the man saw me. He grabbed a spear by the throne and threw it at me.

The throw took me completely by surprise and I instinctively stepped back. The spear flew true and pierced me between the eyes...

Blue sky loomed above me. The angle seemed wrong. Something was different.

Then I realized that I was laying on the ground. At some point I had collapsed and lay on the rough cobble stones of the courtyard.

Rhys and my dad kneeled around me, worried expressions clouding their faces. They were talking to me, but at first no sounds seemed to come from them. Something was wrong with my hearing.

Slowly, the sounds of the world came back to me, gradually getting louder and washing over me.

"Madison, can you hear me?" My dad asked.

I nodded and started to sit up, but stopped when that small movement made the world spin around me. Laying down was safer for the moment.

"What happened?" I asked. My tongue felt thick and my words slurred as I spoke.

"That's what we want to know," Rhys said. His face loomed over me, eyes filled with concern. "One moment you were fine, and the next you fell to the ground, convulsing."

"I touched Thuanar."

"And that's when you collapsed?" asked Kara.

"The whole collapsing thing is blank," I said. "I don't remember it at all. But when I touched him I had a vision."

Complete silence followed my statement. If I hadn't been so shaken up, the looks of confusion on everyone's face would have been really funny.

Dad finally broke the silence. "Ok, let's all just give her some room. There will be plenty of time for questions."

Rhys and Dad helped me into a sitting position. This time the world had the courtesy to not spin about. Kara brought me a bottle of water and after taking a few sips I felt much better.

After a few moments, I told them what happened and the strange vision I saw.

"Has anyone else ever had something like this happen?" I asked.

"Not that I've ever heard of," Dad said. "What about the Binders?" he asked Kara.

Kara shook her head. "I've never heard of anyone having a vision when touching a bound Havoc. I mean, that's the whole point of the binding, isn't it? That the Havoc can't bother anyone."

"Great, I'm the oddball once again," I said. "That seems to be the story of my life."

After a few more minutes I was feeling well enough to stand up. I looked around and saw Thuanar sitting motionless on the cobblestones staring intently at me. His large eyes, full of anger and intelligence, bored into me. Then in a quick movement, Thuanar spun around and walked off in the other direction, clearly dismissing me.

"I think we should get Madison back to the hotel," Rhys said, and Dad immediately agreed.

Thunar was clearly done with me, and I could feel the beginnings of a spectacular headache coming on. I wasn't about to touch him again.

Araceli led us off the cathedral grounds and back towards our hotel.

As we walked, Dad and Rhys both hovered nearby as if I were some Victorian-age woman liable to get the vapors and collapse at any moment.

"I'm fine," I said. "I just have a headache, that's all."

But this was Dad and Rhys we're talking about, and I knew arguing with them was pointless, so I let them hover and didn't make a fuss.

Clack.

Something very small flew past me and hit the wall beside my head. It was just a tiny noise. It was so faint that an ordinary person likely wouldn't have even noticed it. The small something fell to the ground.

In a flash Rhys bent down and picked it up. It appeared to be a needle-like piece of bone about an inch long. The tip of the bone was covered in a yellow tar-like substance. His eyes grew wide with fear.

A second bone shard whizzed through the air, this time it hit the wall just in front of me.

It was a dart. A bone dart.

Both Rhys and my Dad jumped in front of me. It was like one of those movies when the president is under attack and the secret service people dive in front of him to take the bullet.

Only this was a weapon designed for a Berserker.

"What are you doing?" I yelled. I didn't want anyone dying while trying to save me. Especially not those two.

"Get down, Madison," my Dad said. "Someone is trying to kill you."

"What if they're after Rhys?" I asked.

"They're not," said Rhys.

"You don't know that," I said. "You can't possibly know that."

"That's a chance I'm willing to take," said Rhys.

By now I had slipped into a pre-zerk. Dad and Rhys were standing in front of me, but I looked around them and scanned the crowd. My enhanced senses had no problem finding the attacker. He raised a blowgun up to his lips and fired a third bone dart.

In half a heartbeat, I had slipped out from behind Dad and Rhys. In a single fluid motion, I pulled the hat off a passing stranger and used it to knock the flying dart out of the air. I didn't dare use my hand in case it scratched me, and I was guessing that yellow stuff was some kind of poison.

The attacker saw me, and spun around, running away from us and into a crowd.

I took off after him.

"Madison! Don't do it!" yelled Rhys.

There was no way I was going to stop. I could move quickly without looking conspicuous which made me the best candidate to catch this guy.

And I had a few questions for him.

Using my enhanced speed and reflexes, I twisted my way through the crowd faster than humanly possible. I weaved in and out always managing to stay a half step ahead of the moving people and find the path through them.

Unfortunately, getting through the crowd quickly meant some twists and turns which took the attacker out of my sight. By the time I got to where the attacker had been, I could no longer see him. I spun around searching for any sign of him. Farther down the street I caught sight of him pushing his way through the crowd – considerably slower than I could.

Once again, I waded into the crowd, this time being more careful to keep him in sight. I was much better at moving through the crowd, and I began to catch up to him. He looked back over his shoulder, saw me gaining on him, and changed direction, heading for an alley away from the crowds.

I followed him into a small side street and around a corner. My Berserker hearing caught the sound of the blow gun firing another bone dart just as I rounded the corner. I dropped to my knees and bent my body backwards, sliding under the dart. I watched it sail over and harmlessly past me.

I immediately jumped back up to discover I was completely alone in a dead end street.

My attacker had disappeared.

CHAPTER 9

BOYS WILL BE BOYS

T o say that Dad and Rhys were upset with me for running off would be an understatement. It would be like saying that the surface of the sun is warm, or that Joan Rivers looks plastic.

I knew I had scared both of them, but I couldn't have let the attacker go without at least trying to stop him. I was the only one who could access some of my powers without fully 'zerking so I was the natural choice.

I just wished I had caught the attacker.

After Dad and Rhys caught up I continued to look around, trying to figure out where the attacker had gone. It was a dead end with no place to go, but he had somehow just... disappeared. My mind couldn't accept that explanation and kept going in circles looking for some clue I had missed that would show us where he had gone.

Nothing.

Dad and Rhys were both convinced that the attack was a set up.

Someone had known Berserkers would come to investigate what was happening with the seal and had been prepared.

The yellow stuff on the bone dart was a toxin made from some rare plants found only in South America. The toxin would quickly kill an ordinary human. With Berserkers, it messed up their nervous system, causing vivid hallucinations and leaving them almost incapable of voluntary movement. It was the poison of choice for desperate people who wanted to capture a live Berserker to sacrifice on a seal.

And for that reason, Dad made arrangements to fly us home ASAP. It would mean a late-night arrival, but with the attacker still at large, Dad wasn't going to let me take any more chances.

Fortunately, the flight back was completely uneventful. I even slept through most of the final leg back to Portland.

When we got off the plane, I made it through customs quickly. The others had much more interesting travel histories with passports full of visas to exotic places and were more thoroughly questioned.

Once I had my bag, the security officers insisted that I keep moving and exit the customs area. I pulled my bag down a long hallway and through a secure door that opened into the general airport baggage claim.

I was surprised to see a group of familiar faces.

Eric, Aata, and Shing were all there along with three other men I didn't know.

Eric raced up and gave me a huge hug, picking me up and spinning me around. It was definitely over-the-top enthusiastic.

Which was typical Eric.

Once I caught my breath, I gave Aata a hug – but not quite so energetic as the one Eric gave me. Even Shing hugged me, although he did look a little uncomfortable about it.

"Who are your friends?" I asked Eric.

Eric leaned in conspiratorially and in an exaggerated stage whisper said, "They're Berserkers." He put his finger to his lips. "Shhhh."

As much as he could get on my nerves at times, I couldn't help smiling.

"Thanks for the warning," I whispered back. "Do they have names?"

With a huge grin, one of the three stepped forward and made a deep bow that practically folded him in half. He was an extremely tall African man – well over six and a half feet tall. His skin was darker than any other person I had ever seen. He appeared to be in his mid forties and had close cropped, slightly graying hair. The lithe grace of his motions made me think he would be extremely quick for someone his size.

"My name is Davu," he said once he had straightened up. His smile made his eyes crinkle up in crow's feet. He was the oldest looking Berserker I had seen – maybe even older than Shing. How old was he?

The second person appeared about my age. His light brown hair was poker straight and cut long so it partially obscured his face. I could make out a long, straight nose and a rather prominent chin with a cleft in it.

"Pleasure to meet you," he said, in a difficult to understand mumble. "My name's Arthur Cooper." As I took his hand, I noticed he had extremely long, delicate fingers – almost feminine, but I decided not to mention that.

The third person wore cowboy boots, a Stetson hat, and exclusively denim clothing. He looked to be in his early twenties, and his tanned face showed several days' worth of stubble. He made a sweeping bow, removing his hat to reveal dark curly hair. He then took my hand and said, "Name's Josiah. Josiah Smith." His voice had a slight hint of a southern twang in it. He lifted my hand and was about to kiss it when I politely – but firmly – extracted it. He grinned and gave me a wink, completely unabashed.

Another Berserker flirt. Just what we needed.

Well, he wasn't a bad looking guy, but he was so not my type. Besides, I had Rhys.

A few minutes later Dad, Rhys, and Kara exited from customs.

"Scotty!" Eric shouted, and gave my dad a huge bear hug. Dad rolled his eyes.

The next few minutes were full of hugs, bows, and handshakes as everyone greeted each other.

I did notice that Kara and Aata were very careful to avoid each other. They did such a good job that it was glaringly obvious how aware they were of each other.

It broke my heart to see them like this. I just wished they could find a way to make it work. My dad and mom had made it work. They had been happy together.

Well, maybe that wasn't the best example.

***

As soon as we got home, Dad went to bed. He stumbled into his room and disappeared. Unlike me, he hadn't slept on the plane and was exhausted. I had slept enough that despite the late hour I wasn't ready to go to sleep when we got home. Instead I unpacked and put everything away. Once that was done, I crawled into bed and read a book.

Once my eyelids started to droop, I turned out the lights and closed my eyes. I was just starting to drift to sleep when I felt the unmistakable sensation of someone 'zerking. My eyes flew open, sleep forgotten. Was one of the Berserkers in danger?

Within seconds I had jumped out of bed and yanked on some jeans and a blouse. I was about to go downstairs when I heard something hit my bedroom window.

I pushed back the curtains and threw open the window... just in time to get hit in the head with a very small rock.

"Sorry!" said a voice from below.

I looked down and saw Eric, holding a handful of gravel, looking sheepish. Next to him were two of the new Berserkers, Josiah – in full 'zerk – and Arthur, looking sullen, with his hands jammed into his pockets.

"What do you want?" I hissed.

"Can Madison come out and play?" asked Eric, giving me his

most insolent grin.

"It's after one O'clock," I said. "Sane people are in bed now."

"Ah," said Eric. "That would explain why I'm out of bed. Come on, don't be so dutiful. You need a little insanity in your life."

I did my best not to react to Eric's goad. I knew him well enough now to know when he was trying to push my buttons. I wasn't going to take the bait.

"It's late," I said. "I'm going to bed." I reached up and started to close the window.

"Come on," said Eric. "Don't make me get out my boom box and start playing sappy 80's love songs until you come out."

Despite my best efforts to keep a straight face I let out a laugh. Great, that would only encourage him. How could he have possibly known how much I loved the movie "Say Anything?" I was torn between wanting to keep laughing and the desire to yell at him to leave me alone.

I was about to tell Eric that it would take more than that to get me out when I felt two pairs of strong hands grab me and pull me through the window.

For an instant I was falling, and instinctively I 'zerked – only to be caught a second later by three sets of Berserker hands and gently set on my feet.

I whirled to see who had pulled me out of the window. Aata and Davu were perched on the roof to either side of my bedroom waving at me. I hadn't realized they were there because I had assumed that Josiah was the only source of the 'zerking.

Aata and Davu jumped down from the second story, landing with easy grace. Aata put his arm around me.

"Come on," he said. "Don't be mad. It was the only way we were going to get you out of the house for your initiation."

Initiation? That didn't sound so good. The word conjured images of sorority hazing rituals designed to humiliate the pledges. No thanks, not my thing.

"Yeah, well, I'm going to pass all the same."

Eric rolled his eyes in exasperation. "Come on, Miss Perfect. Don't be so uptight. You've been hanging around Rhys too long. All his responsible behavior is rubbing off on you."

"You say that like it's a bad thing."

"Only because it is."

By now I was surrounded by Eric, Aata, Davu, Josiah, and Arthur, and I could tell I wasn't going to be able to talk my way out of this. I didn't think they would resort to actually kidnapping me, but I didn't completely rule out that possibility either.

I had no desire to participate in whatever initiation they had planned, but I could tell this was important to Eric, and despite his crazy bravado, I knew he wouldn't deliberately put me in danger. I could forcefully tell them to go away, and most likely they would. Or I could give in and see what Eric was up to.

With a pronounced sigh, I said, "What did you have in mind?"

Eric grinned. "You'll see."

Before I knew what was happening, we had all piled into the Range Rover – a snug fit – and were heading up the Columbia River gorge.

When we pulled into the deserted parking lot of Multnomah Falls, a huge waterfall and a popular tourist attraction, I had serious second thoughts.

"You're not thinking what I'm afraid you're thinking?" I asked.

"Oh, yes he is," said Davu.

Multnomah Falls was actually two waterfalls on top of each other. The first waterfall dropped into a large pool five hundred and forty feet below. The pool emptied off a cliff into another pool seventy feet farther down. The second fall was spanned by a cement bridge that made for a rather picturesque scene.

We climbed out of the car and 'zerked, easily jumping the chains that blocked the trail leading to the falls. I had hiked to the top before and it consisted of dozens of steep switchbacks. Back then I had to stop and rest several times, but tonight – or was that this morning? – we reached the summit in a matter of minutes.

I looked at the cascading water tumbling over the edge. This wasn't my first time at the falls, but looking at the pool below with the idea of jumping off made the drop look higher than I remembered.

Davu, Arthur, Josiah, and Aata were already wading into the water, wrestling around, each trying to pick the others up and throw them over the falls.

I stayed on the edge of the path, reluctant to get into the water as the idea of getting wet while fully dressed had an appeal far to the left of zero on a number line. Eric stayed by my side, watching the antics of the other Berserkers. After several minutes of a crazy free-for-all, Davu, Arthur, and Aata teamed up to throw Josiah over the edge.

With a whoop and a "Yee-haw!" he flew over the side, a glowing comet slashing through the air to land in the pool below with a huge splash. I held my breath waiting to see if he was okay. Within seconds he emerged from the water whooping and hollering like it was an amusement park ride.

In unison, I saw three sets of eyes turn from watching Josiah below, to where Eric and I stood on the side.

"Oh no," I said, and started to back up.

Before I could go anywhere, I felt Eric's grip on my arm, holding me in place, a huge grin splitting his face.

As if that were the cue, the other three Berserkers rushed towards me, grabbed my arms and legs and dragged me towards the falls.

I thrashed and yelled, having no desire to go over the edge. It must have reached a critical level because Eric leaned down and whispered in my ear. "I promise you won't get hurt. Relax and let go."

"I'm not worried about that," I said. And I wasn't. I had been a Berserker long enough to know I was pretty sturdy when 'zerking. "I just don't want to get wet."

That was clearly the wrong thing to say.

Eric laughed and with a single heave, they threw me over the edge.

I flew through the air, speeding downward. A strange sense of duality hit me. I felt like I was speeding towards the water below, and yet simultaneously moving in slow motion. My adrenalin surged and the world became even brighter and the colors more vivid.

It felt wonderful!

I splashed into the first pool and made a split second decision. Without surfacing, I swam behind the rushing water so I wouldn't be visible from above. Safely hidden, I waited until I heard Eric's panicked yell. A few seconds later he splashed into the pool just in front of me.

Seizing the opportunity for revenge, I swam up behind Eric and pinned his arms at his sides.

"Madison, you're all-" he began, but was quickly cut off as I dunked him under the water and then lifted him into the air, throwing him over the edge of the second drop.

Eric flailed awkwardly as he splashed down, sputtering to catch his breath from the lower pool where Josiah laughed and dunked Eric back under the moment he came up for air.

Clearly, I wasn't the only one who wanted a bit of revenge.

As the other Berserkers landed in the first pool with me, I decided it would be better to jump of my own accord than to have them tackle me again.

This time I executed a smooth dive with a couple of flips and twists in it. I had always liked watching the divers in the Olympics, but I had never dared to try any of their moves. Now the movement came easily and naturally to me.

With hardly any splash, I landed in the lower pool and surfaced near Eric. He glared at me.

"That was devious and deceitful, Madison. You made me think

something had gone wrong and then took advantage of me." His stern look morphed into his patented mischievous smile. "I must be rubbing off on you."

We jumped off the falls several more times before I started getting too cold. Running up the trail helped keep me warm, and the 'zerk seemed to moderate my body temperature, but after a while, it was draining to keep the 'zerk going, and I was ready to be done.

To my pleasant surprise Eric had come prepared. The back of the Range Rover was filled with towels, blankets and coats. There was even a full set of new clothes for me to change into.

I found a secluded spot and changed, coming back to find Eric sitting on the ground with a blanket wrapped around him.

"Care to join me?" he asked.

The other Berserkers were already heading back up to the top for more, so I sat down beside him, well out of cuddle range.

Of course that lasted for about three seconds. He immediately scooted over and tried to wrap the blanket around me as well. It was like one of Amy's devious plans, but with all the subtlety of a rampaging elephant.

I held up an arm to stop him before it happened. "Eric, I don't think that's a good idea."

He gave me an exaggerated expression of hurt. "You besmirch my honor, Madison," he said and retracted the arm holding out the open blanket.

"Besmirch?"

"To charge falsely or with malicious-"

"I know the definition," I said. "I just don't think I've ever heard anyone actually use it in conversation before."

"Well, lucky for both of us I'm not just anyone," Eric said. "Now, you are wet and cold, and I am trying to be a gentleman and offer you some warmth." He held out the blanket again. "No strings attached."

Unfortunately, Eric was right. I was kind of cold and I could feel the beginning of my teeth wanting to chatter. With a sigh, I let Eric wrap half of the blanket around me.

"How much longer do you think they are going to be?" I asked. One of the Berserkers – I couldn't tell who from so far down – did a swan dive into the lower falls.

"I don't know. I say let them have their fun. It's not very often that we get to socialize with any of the seven."

"Rhys seems to think they're more interested in showing each other up than in catching Havocs," I said.

"He would." Eric rolled his eyes. "There's more to being a Berserker than searching for Havocs. We've spent the last several months doing that and it's time for a break. Sure, the seven like to play, but they're in a bit of a different situation."

"How so?"

"Most of the time, the idiots who think it's a good idea to free the Havocs don't bother with the seven because it's next to impossible to kill them all at the same time. Especially since at any given time there is one who is always in hiding. The location is constantly changing and is only known by one other person. That means they are rarely targeted like we are. Plus, the Havocs who do get free generally come after one of us five. Mostly you for now."

"But don't you think they should be helping you capture the other Havocs? Isn't that part of the Berserker's duty?"

Eric shook his head slowly. "I knew it was dangerous leaving you here with Rhys. Clearly his stick-in-the-muddery has worn off on you." He pulled back a bit and turned so he was facing me. "Can't you see? There is no duty. You can't have duty if you don't make a commitment, and believe me, I didn't sign up for this." He took a deep breath. "Let's talk about something else. What's been going on at school? Is Ginger still giving you a hard time? I have some new ideas on how to get back at her if she is."

For the next few minutes I gave him the update on what had happened, careful to avoid any mention that I was dating Rhys. I told him about the attack in the alley, about casting the haze on Josh and his renewed affections, and about the Azark I killed on the catwalk in the auditorium.

Rather than looking shocked at the news of Berserker assassins summoned by Binders, he looked more amused than anything.

"Well that's just not fair," Eric said. "I go out looking for a bit of adventure hunting Osadyn and instead all the excitement ends up being here, with you." There was something different about the way Eric said this. It started off with his usual mocking tone, but by the end, he was gazing into my eyes like we were long lost lovers reunited at last.

"Yeah, it's non-stop excitement with me around," I said, trying to add a bit of humor to an increasingly awkward conversation.

"You don't understand how special you are," Eric said, reaching out and holding my hand tightly in his.

Clearly my efforts to lighten the situation had backfired. Instead of taking the hint that I didn't want to have a serious conversation about us, Eric had interpreted my comment as misplaced insecurity in need of reassurance. He seemed poised on the verge of professing undying love to me.

Not the conversation I wanted to have right now. Or ever, really.

"While I was gone, I couldn't stop thinking about you," he said. "About us. About the picnic up in the gorge."

"You mean the time when I almost killed you when I shot up with my EpiPen?"

The only reaction this elicited was a brief smile. Clearly, Eric had been planning this conversation for a while and subtle hints were not sufficient to derail it now.

"About how you and I connected that day. How I was able to confide in you and tell you things I had never told another living soul. That was something special."

Crap! What was I supposed to do? I could see where this was going. Should I cut him off before he said something we both regretted or let him talk and then gently tell him I wasn't interested?

"We have a connection," he continued. "There is no denying that."

"Look, Eric, I–"

"Shhh." He pressed a finger to my lips.

Did he just shush me?

I'm sure it was intended to be romantic or something, but it felt condescending. Was what I had to say unimportant?

He leaned in for a kiss, and in that instant I knew I couldn't let this go on any longer. I held up a hand and gently stopped him from getting close enough to kiss me.

Eric's eyes fluttered open, surprise and confusion clouding his features. "What's wrong?"

I pulled the blanket off of me. "It's this, Eric," I said, indicating the two of us. "I think you're a great guy, but I don't think you and I are right for each other."

A brief look of pain flashed across Eric's face, only to be replaced a second later with a mocking grin. It happened quickly, but not quickly enough that I could convince myself he wasn't hurting.

"Well, you can't blame a guy for trying," he said. He stood up and gave an exaggerated stretch. "I'm going to take a few more jumps."

He 'zerked and ran off into the night, his glow disappearing behind the trees as he raced up the switchbacks.

I watched him disappear up the trail, my thoughts in an uproar. What had just happened? I so hadn't been ready for Eric to make a move on me.

Eric arrived at the top of the falls and began dunking Josiah. Aata and Davu teamed up and threw Arthur over the edge. As I watched Eric playing with the Berserkers, I had a feeling that what had just happened was going to have lasting consequences – ones that would make me regret ever coming out here tonight.

CHAPTER 10

FROM BAD TO WORSE

The ride home was full of laughter and put downs as the Berserkers bantered back and forth, more like middle school boys than exceptionally old men. Did living for hundreds of years cause you to regress back to pre-pubescent behaviors?

Eric laughed and joked with the others, but he didn't say a single word to me on the way home. He didn't glare or give me hurt looks. He just acted as if I weren't even there. Clearly I had hurt him tonight, but what else could I have done? I loved Rhys, so kissing someone else wasn't even an option – that's not the kind of girl I was.

By the time Eric pulled up at my house, it was almost six in the morning. The other Berserkers all gave me enthusiastic hugs and goodbyes. Eric just stared out the window until I climbed out of the car, and he drove away before I even made it up the driveway.

I 'zerked and climbed up the outside of the house to sneak in through my bedroom window – I really didn't want my dad to know that I had been gone all night while he slept. I quickly changed and crawled back into bed. By this time my eyes were burning from staying up so long, and I lay my head down on the pillow and let blissful sleep overcome me.

***

Monday morning at school, I was surprised by a squealing Amy running towards me as I entered the building with Rhys. In her enthusiasm, she practically tackled me in the hallway.

"Guess what, guess what, guess what?" she said, bouncing up and down with excitement.

"Aliens came and brought us the cure for all known diseases?"

My answer didn't even make Amy blink. "No, even better! Josh and I are going to Prom!" She squealed again, even higher pitched.

Prom? Was it that time already? I guess with all the Berserker and Binder things, plus the play, and monsters trying to kill me, I had lost track of the school social calendar.

Why hadn't Rhys asked me yet?

Before I could say anything, Rhys put a hand on my shoulder. "It looks like you and Amy need some girl time," he said. "I'll be at my locker." He reached down, gave my hand a squeeze, and then disappeared into the crowd.

"So what happened?" I asked, turning my attention back to Amy. I was trying to be a good, supportive friend and be excited for her, but it was hard to match Amy's level of excitement about Prom. Especially since I hadn't been asked yet.

"OK, so I don't know what happened between you and Josh, but after the play, I could totally tell he was on the rebound. So I made plans with him to spend time together during Spring Break. We went down to Riverside Trail – I know total make out spot, right? – and we talked for the longest time and he asked me to Prom! Then we kissed and it was the most amazing..."

Amy continued on for several more minutes. I was honestly happy for her. Having Josh date Amy made my life much less awkward with Rhys. Of course, just as Josh is finally out of the picture, Eric comes back, but I didn't even want to think about him right now.

A flash of red caught my attention as Amy continued on about Prom. Ginger Johnson pushed her way through the crowd and stood right by Amy and me, clearly within the conversation perimeter.

"What do you want?" Amy asked. The look of hate between the two of them was palpable. Which, given that Amy was going to Prom with Josh, made perfect sense.

"For you to get lost," said Ginger. "I want to talk with Madison. Alone." She fixed Amy with her well-used nasty glare.

"Listen, Ginger, I–" Amy began.

I put a hand on Amy's shoulder. Given that Ginger had seen me 'zerk and had been attacked by a monster, I figured I should at least listen to what she had to say.

"I've got this Amy," I said. "It's OK."

Amy gave me a long, searching look before shrugging her

shoulders. "If that's what you want." She threw one last glare at Ginger before flipping her hair back and strutting down the hall.

Ginger watched her walk down the hall for a moment before rolling her eyes and turning to me.

"She's going to Prom with Josh?" she asked.

Well, this wasn't exactly how I thought the conversation would start. "That's what she told me."

"Whatever," Ginger said, and she folded her arms across her chest. "I'm so over him. He had his chance and blew it. If he wants to commit social seppuku by dating her that's his business."

"Seppuku?"

Ginger waved a dismissive hand. "I'm not your dictionary. Look it up if your vocabulary isn't up to the challenge."

I was so shocked that for a moment I didn't say anything at all. Ginger was insulting my vocabulary? I bit back a slew of nasty retorts and focused on repressing my urge to pummel her.

"Did you come here to do something besides insult me?" I asked. "Because you usually don't seem too fussy about doing that in public."

"True," she said, looking around furtively to see that no one was listening in. "I just wanted to tell you–" she paused and took a deep breath. "I just wanted to say thanks for saving me from that monster."

Who was this girl? She wasn't acting like the Ginger I knew. I was so used to dealing with her insults and threats that I was completely at a loss how to respond to a simple thank-you.

"Look," she said, "that Scottish girl, Kara, told me what you've been doing to protect us from those creatures. I have several uncles in the military, so I can respect the way you put your life on the line to defend others." She reached out and shook my hand. "Don't worry; I'll keep your secret."

***

That night after Berserker training, Rhys and I went out to the back deck to cool off and look at the stars. We sat together on the porch swing, me leaning back with Rhys' arms wrapped around me. The swing was set up against the back of the house and wasn't visible from any of the windows, so we had decided to enjoy the privacy and take a few minutes to be together.

"This feels great," I said, enjoying the sensation of him holding me close. "I could stay here forever."

"You might get hungry," Rhys said. "Forever is a pretty long time."

I reached back and playfully smacked him on the back of the head. "You know what I mean."

"I do. Believe me, I do."

"I still can't believe Amy and Josh are going to Prom together," I said. I'd had the entire day to process through the news, but it still seemed incredible to me. Just over a week ago, Josh had kissed me in the middle of the play and now he was going to Prom with my best friend.

"Does it bother you?" Rhys asked.

I thought about it for a minute. It had been several months since Josh and I had broken up, so it was past the statute of limitations on how long you should wait before dating your best friend's ex. Technically, it hadn't been that long since Josh was trying to get me back, but in a way I was grateful that Amy was there to remove some of the awkwardness. There may have been a teeny tiny part of me that was secretly jealous, but that was mostly because she would be going to Prom and I wouldn't.

"I'm not jealous that she's going out with Josh," I said, "but I am a little envious that she gets to go to Prom while we have to hide our relationship from my dad and the other Berserkers. It just kind of sucks, you know?"

Rhys inhaled deeply. "Yeah, it does."

"I just wish we could be together," I said, "and not have to hide this from my family like some twisted Romeo and Juliet and superhero mash-up story."

Rhys laughed. "Their powers brought them together, but their families keep them apart," he intoned in a passable imitation of an announcer's voice.

"Exactly," I said and leaned my head back for a kiss.

Rhys gently pressed his lips to mine. Everything else faded away as I simply enjoyed the feel of his lips on mine and pretended that we were just two teenagers stealing kisses away from prying eyes – no powers, no Havocs, no saving the world.

Until I felt someone 'zerk.

Instantly we both broke off the kiss. The person 'zerking had been close by. It only took a second to find the source.

Eric stood on the grass just off the deck, a look of mingled horror and despair flashing across his face. He had apparently come into the back yard through the gate at the side of the house.

Although he was 'zerking and his glow obscured his features, his eyes fixed on mine and for a moment I could feel his sense of betrayal. The utter despair and hopelessness that radiated from him was enough to make me nauseated.

"Eric, I..." I began, but I had no words of comfort to give him.

Eric made a strange, strangled noise and then ran. In an instant he was gone, leaving nothing but the bright afterimage of his glow burned into my eyes.

"I'm going after him," said Rhys, and in a heartbeat he had 'zerked and gone.

I sat alone on the porch swing, waiting for Rhys to return and wishing that I had never gotten out of bed today. What was I supposed to do?

I loved Rhys, not Eric.

The problem was that I had seen the other side of Eric. He had let me see past the jokes and bravado to the man who hated himself for the horrible things he had done, who had loved a woman so deeply that her death had scarred him forever.

He had trusted me, confided in me. Now that trust was gone, and I had a feeling that nothing would ever make it whole again. Even though I hadn't done anything wrong, I felt as if I had somehow betrayed him and violated his confidence. Intellectually, I knew it was a stupid thought born out of empathy and sorrow for his pain, but it was a hard feeling to repress.

Minutes passed, then an hour, and still Rhys hadn't returned. I was about to go back inside when I felt a Berserker approaching.

Rhys came around the side of the house and turned off the 'zerk. He shook his head in answer to my unasked question.

"I couldn't find him," he said. "He's gone."

* * *

For the next several days the Berserkers searched for Eric. His disappearance wasn't something we could keep hidden, although we didn't tell them why he had run off. I was pretty sure Mallika and Kara suspected, but thankfully they didn't ask or tell.

On Thursday after school, Rhys and I went to the Berserker house for my Binder training. The house was unnaturally subdued, and the atmosphere felt extremely tense, as if we were all holding our breath and waiting.

Kara and I went into the mirrored room, but once we got in there I could see that something was wrong. She looked tired and even more pale than usual. Red blotches covered her neck and she seemed to be having difficulty breathing.

I helped her over to a chair and made her sit down. She looked like she was about to pass out.

"What's wrong?" I asked.

At first she didn't respond, and her head lolled on her shoulders as if she had just lost consciousness. I gently patted her cheeks until she opened her eyes.

"Are you ok?" I asked. "What's going on?"

"Eric. Something is really wrong with him."

"What do you mean? What kind of wrong? Is he in danger?"

Kara shook her head. "I don't think so, at least not yet." She seemed to gather her strength and sat up straighter. "I can feel him through our connection. I always could when he was close, but not like this. He's in pain, Madison. I've never felt him upset like this." She reached out a hand and touched my arm. "I think he's looking for Osadyn."

My insides suddenly went cold. The moment she said it, I knew it was true. This is how he dealt with pain – drowning it out by seeking danger.

"But he won't be able to find Osadyn, right?" I asked. "They've been searching for months without any luck, so there's no way he could find him by himself."

But I could tell from the frightened expression on Kara's face that my theory was flawed.

"It doesn't work that way," she said. "When Berserkers are in a group the Havocs are more likely to run than fight. Three or more Berserkers together are too much of a threat. A single Berserker half out of his mind would be too tempting to pass up."

The ride back to my house with Rhys was pretty quiet. I didn't want to talk about Eric, but right now everything else felt trivial and superficial.

The lights were on and my dad was sitting on a rocking chair on the front porch when we pulled into the driveway. When I saw the look on Dad's face, I knew something was wrong. My mind raced through all the possibilities as I jumped out of the Rover and ran up the driveway.

"What's wrong?" I asked.

But Dad hardly seemed to notice me. His eyes were fixed on something behind me, and he strode past me to Rhys.

Then Dad pulled back his fist and punched Rhys in the face.

I heard a crack. Rhys staggered backwards, clearly taken off guard.

For a moment I was too stunned to do anything but watch, but when Dad pulled back his fist for another hit, I moved in to pull him away.

"I trusted you!" Dad shouted at Rhys. I pulled him back, easily slipping into a pre-zerk. "And this is how you repay me, by seducing my daughter?"

Cold fear enveloped me. Dad knew.

Almost immediately, the fear was replaced by anger. I never had been very good at letting people tell me what to do, and this was no exception.

"What are you talking about?" I shouted. "No one seduced me."

"This."

From out of his pocket Dad pulled a photograph showing Rhys and I kissing beside my locker. We hadn't kissed very much at school – both of us were rather private – but clearly someone had photographed one of our rare public moments and sent the evidence to my dad.

"You disgust me," Dad said, and I had to tighten my grip to keep him from lunging at Rhys. "You may look like a teenager, but we both know you're really an old man."

Rhys recoiled as Dad hurled accusations, each one seeming to cause him physical pain. His eyes had widened and I could see that this was exactly the kind of reaction he had feared.

"Scottie, I..."

"You're what? Sorry? Sorry doesn't cut it. You crossed a boundary, and we both know it." Dad shuddered with barely contained rage. "You know, I can still remember all the talks we had back in the day about how you had lost your soulmate and would never love again. Too bad I didn't know what kind of sleaze you would turn into; I wouldn't have bothered to listen to your lies."

"Stop it!" I shouted. "Stop saying these awful things that just aren't true. You have no idea what's going on and you have no right to judge."

Dad's eyes bulged, and I could see I hit a nerve. "Judge? You think this is about judging you? This is about protecting you from a two-hundred-year-old lecher." He glared at Rhys. "Go away and don't ever come back. I forbid you to be with my daughter."

Forbid? Good luck with that.

And like a switch being thrown, my anger disappeared, replaced by a cold resolution.

"Why don't you go home, Rhys," I said. "I think my dad and I need to have a talk."

"Madison, I can't leave you to deal with this by yourself. This involves both of us."

I wanted to reach out and hold him. Embrace him. To unsay all the horrible things Dad had said. But now wasn't the time. I had to be strong now to ensure that we had a tomorrow together.

"It does involve both of us," I said. "But right now this isn't about you."

"It's not?" Rhys looked from me to my dad as if seeking clarification.

"Nope, this is about my dad and me and trust."

After Rhys left I finally let go of Dad.

"I don't blame you, Madison," he began.

"You can't forbid me from seeing Rhys," I said, interrupting him.

Dad's eyes narrowed. "Watch me."

"Correction. You can forbid all you want, but you can't stop me from seeing him. You can't stop me from being with him. You can't stop me from loving him."

Dad opened his mouth to respond, but I cut him off.

"How old were you when you first met Mom?"

It was extremely satisfying to see the color drain out of Dad's face. "That's completely beside the point."

"What are you talking about? It's completely the point. Come on. How old were you? Two hundred? Three hundred?"

"Three hundred and seventy nine," Dad said, his voice hardly a whisper. "But it was a different time, different circumstances."

"Really? Because it sounds like a double standard to me."

"You're too young to understand."

"I understand perfectly. It was fine when you did it, but now that I've found someone who makes me happy, you want to make my life miserable."

Dad started to speak, then shut his mouth and took a deep breath. "You're my daughter and you live in my house. I have the right to impose rules, and right now I forbid you from seeing Rhys or going over to his house again."

There was that word again – forbid. I hate that word.

"And how am I supposed to learn my powers? What about my responsibility as a Berserker and a Binder? Do I just ignore those now, too? Think through what you're asking me to do. This isn't about Rhys, or his age, or anything like that. It's about you not knowing when to let go. You can get all uber-possessive and controlling, but this isn't about me. It's about your issues."

I turned around and walked back into the house.

***

The next morning Rhys didn't pick me up for school. I kept waiting, hoping that he wouldn't let what happened scare him off, but finally it was too late for me to stall any more. I pulled out my keys and hopped into Mom's Jetta, my anger causing me to drive much faster than was probably safe.

But when I got to school, Rhys wasn't there. I searched the

hallways, but he was nowhere to be found. I called the Berserker house, but no one picked up.

I passed through school in a haze, eating lunch alone and hardly speaking to anyone. My mind raced with thoughts of Rhys and what he might be thinking right now. It had been difficult enough to get him to accept his feelings for me, how much harder would it be now for us to have a relationship? I knew he loved me, but I was deathly afraid that Dad's reaction would make him do something stupid and noble like leaving me alone to get over him.

As soon as school ended, I jumped into Mom's car and sped to the Berserker house. Rhys might be willing to abide by Dad's edict of separation, but I wasn't. I was his daughter, and it was my duty to ignore unreasonable rules and restrictions.

I pressed the doorbell and held my breath, the seconds crawling by. My heart pounded and I wanted to bang on the door, yelling for Rhys to open it up, but that seemed a bit overly dramatic.

To my delight Rhys opened the door. I threw myself at him, knocking him back several steps, and gave him the tightest hug of my life, burying my face in his chest.

"You're still here," I said, relief flooding through me.

But I could tell something was wrong.

Usually hugging Rhys was like being wrapped in a warm, soft blanket. This time it felt like I was hugging a block of cement, cold and unyielding.

I pulled back to look at him. "What's wrong?" I asked. But even as the question left my lips, I knew the answer.

"We can't do this," Rhys said. "You can't be here. We can't be together. Your dad was very clear on that point." He reached a hand up and absently rubbed his jaw where Dad had hit him. His Berserker powers had kept him from being physically hurt, but it was clear that Dad's punch had done far more damage than I had feared.

"Don't worry about my dad," I said. "He'll come around. It's just a matter of time."

"I don't think so. I've known Scottie for a long time and I've never seen him blow up like that."

I shrugged, trying to lighten up the mood. "Well, that's because you've never known him when he had a teenage daughter. These days that kind of reaction is pretty standard. The best thing to do is to ignore his outburst and wait for him to come around. He'll thank us for ignoring him when it's over."

Rhys took a step back, removing himself from my arms. "It's not that simple."

Slowly, I let my arms fall to my side now that I had nothing to hold on to.

"See, that's where you're wrong," I said, trying to keep the note of hurt out of my voice. "It's exactly that simple. This is about you and me – no one else."

"I'm sorry, Madison, but we can't be together. Not if it's going to drive a rift between you and your father. I love you too much to do that."

A strange buzzing filled my head, making it hard to think. "You love me too much to be with me? How does that make any sense?" I asked. I could hear frustration starting to rise in my voice.

"It's that—"

But I never did find out what his reasoning was. His words were cut off as a horrific shriek pierced the air. We ran up stairs to find Kara thrashing about on her bed, sweat beading her face. Her eyes were glazed and distant.

"What's going on?" I asked. "Is she sick?"

"I don't know," Rhys said, reaching down to touch her forehead. "She's not hot, so no fever."

Kara let out another piercing shriek. "No!" she screamed. "No! I didn't mean to! Couldn't control."

"What's going on?" Mallika asked. She strode across the room, breathing heavily, her expression dark and serious. She took one look at Kara and the color drained from her face.

Instantly, she sat beside Kara and wrapped her arms around her. "Shhhh, child. It will be all right."

But Kara wouldn't stay still. She thrashed around, growing more violent, screaming out sentences completely disconnected from reality.

Her convulsions grew more violent. One wildly swinging fist hit Mallika in the face, giving her a bloody nose.

"No!" she screamed. "No, Eric. Don't do it!"

Despite her bloody nose, Mallika grabbed Kara by the shoulders and shook her.

"Kara!" she yelled. "Kara, what is Eric doing?"

Kara's eyes rolled up into her head. "Killing the people. Hundreds of them. Can't stop the rage!"

My heart seemed to die in my chest. "Is this now?" I asked. I couldn't believe he would kill people. Not after what he had been through in the army.

Mallika took a deep breath. "I don't know," she said. "Has he killed people in the past?"

I nodded. "Back before he understood what it meant to be a Berserker, he was soldier and used his powers to kill thousands of enemy troops."

Rhys looked stricken. "How do you know that?"

"Eric told me," I said. "You and my dad found him and convinced him to not kill with his powers, but he was afraid to tell you how many people he had already killed. He would never come out and say it, but I can tell it haunts him to this day."

"He never told us," Rhys said. He looked like he was going to be sick. "He kept it to himself all these years."

Kara sat bolt upright, her eyes focused on me. She reached out and tenderly took my hand. "I'm sorry," she said. "I'm so, so sorry. I love you."

My first instinct was to pull my hand away, but Kara held it tightly, and I didn't want to upset her any more than she already was, so I left it there.

Without warning, Kara shuddered and flopped back down, convulsing wildly. Then the convulsions stopped. Kara blinked several times as if trying to clear her vision, and when she finished, she seemed to be herself again, her eyes now bright and clear.

"He's gone," she said, in a voice so low it was almost a whisper. "Eric's gone feral."

Then she passed out.

***

The next hour flew by in a flurry of panicked preparation. If Eric had gone feral, he would have to be stopped – at any cost. The problem was, no one knew where he had gone. As his Binder, Kara was psychically bonded to him, but she remained unconscious except for a few brief spells of incoherent screaming.

When I asked how we would ever find him, Rhys said: "Don't worry, if she's right, we'll know soon enough." He turned on the TV to the local NBC channel.

Less than an hour later the programming was interrupted by a breaking-news story about a tragedy in Brookings-Harbor. Someone – or some animal – the reports weren't clear, had attacked and killed dozens of people during a festival at the local marina.

It wasn't hard to put two and two together.

Mallika went pale and put a hand to her mouth.

"Oh, Eric," she said.

"We leave in ten minutes," Rhys said, and he and the other Berserkers began making final preparations.

***

I watched the Berserkers leave with dread and worry gnawing at my insides. How could Eric have killed all those people? Would Rhys and the other Berserkers be able to stop him?

It frustrated me that I was being left behind. I had begged, argued, cajoled, and pleaded for them to let me go, but the consensus from the other Berserkers was clear – it was too dangerous. I was too new and hadn't been trained for the possibility of fighting a feral Berserker.

"Isn't it dangerous to be left alone if someone is really out to kill me?" I asked.

Rhys blinked in surprise.

"She makes a good point," said Aata.

"No," said Mallika. "Putting you into certain danger to avoid the possibility of danger doesn't make sense." She looked over at me and gave me a sad smile. "And given the circumstances, I'm afraid your presence may just push Eric farther over the edge."

There wasn't much I could do in the face of a unanimous decision. If Eric had been there, I knew he would have let me go, but since he was the source of the problem, he wasn't exactly there to back me up.

As I watched the story unfold on the news, I felt dead inside. I should have been horrified by Eric's rampage, but instead I was numb. Looking at the destruction, all I could think was: How could this have happened? They had told me that Berserkers sometimes went feral, but everyone said it hadn't happened for hundreds of years.

Now I come along and it happens within a few months. Was it my fault, then? Did this happen because Eric saw me kissing Rhys? I could still see the look of betrayal and hurt in his eyes before he ran off.

I doubted I would ever forget it.

***

For two days I fumbled through my routine, my mind completely preoccupied. What was happening with Eric? Was he still alive? Were he and Rhys battling for their lives while I was stuck in school struggling to care about Physics? What if my presence might have been the tipping point between success and failure?

I spent the majority of my afternoons at the Berserker house helping Mallika care for Kara, despite my dad's orders to never go there again. I didn't care – this was bigger than his dislike of Rhys.

The first night I had come back after spending all afternoon and evening at the Berserker house, Dad had confronted me about it, once again forbidding me to go there. But I simply stood there, not saying anything. Eventually he had gotten tired of yelling, and I had my chance to speak.

"Don't worry, Dad," I said. "Rhys isn't there. He's with the rest of the Berserkers trying to prevent Eric from killing people."

Dad's expression changed from anger to shock. "What?"

"He's gone feral, Dad. He attacked all those people in Brookings-Harbor." I could feel tears welling up. I had been so good about keeping my emotions in check for the past two days, but somehow, telling it to Dad made it all hit home, and I could feel the emotions bubbling up, hot and unwanted.

"Oh, Madison," Dad said when he saw my tears. He tried to pull me in for a hug, but I jerked away and ran upstairs. I spent the rest of the night in my room trying to get rid of all those stupid tears. But no matter how much I cried, I never seemed to run out.

***

The next morning I woke up early, a shooting pain in my head. In my mind flashed a picture of a green hill surrounded by forest, and a beautiful woman with long curly red hair dancing in the sun.

The image shattered and was replaced by a shadowy battlefield. Soldiers wearing old US uniforms dashed from tree to tree, firing at the opposing army. The boy next to me fell to the ground as his head disappeared, a jagged stump remaining at his neck.

Nausea overwhelmed me; a hot, thick blanket, covering me. Smothering me. I rolled off the bed and vomited onto the floor.

Even as I threw up, more images flooded my mind. Faces, places, events all jumped into my thoughts with such speed that they became a whirling blur. My head felt like it was going to burst.

And then they stopped.

I lay panting on the floor beside the pool of vomit, a horrible feeling of dread inside me. Something was terribly wrong.

The clock said it was two thirty in the morning, but I could only focus on one thing: I needed to get to the Berserker house.

Still in my pajamas, I grabbed my purse and ran downstairs. I dashed out the front door, not even bothering to close it behind me. Without a backward glance, I jumped into Mom's Jetta and sped off.

Not caring if I got a ticket, I drove faster than I had ever done before. Adrenaline coursed through me, and I was pre-zerking without even trying. My heightened reflexes helped me stay on the road and push the car to its limits.

I squealed up the driveway, dread pulsing through me. I leapt out of the car and pounded on the front door, yelling for Mallika to open up.

After what felt like a half dozen eternities, I saw a light turn on upstairs. Movement at window showed me that someone had just looked outside.

I didn't stop pounding until I heard the locks turning. The door cracked open, and the wide eyes of Mallika peered out at me through the tiny opening.

"Madison?" she said. "What's going on? Why are you here?"

I pushed past her and started up the stairs.

"Something's wrong," I said. "Something's happened with Kara and Eric."

Mallika's mouth hung open in an exaggerated parody of surprise, but only for a moment. She closed her mouth and with an expression of grim determination followed me up the stairs.

I didn't bother knocking on Kara's door. This was too important, and if my horrible feeling was right, it would have been a pointless exercise.

There on the bed, twisted into an awkward position, her body tangled in the sheets, lay Kara.

Unmoving and unbreathing.

I dashed across the room, but even as I tried to wake her, I knew she was dead. Her body was still warm, her death too recent to have gone cold.

CHAPTER 11

HATEFUL

I didn't cry. I wanted too, but I was in too much shock. My eyes burned from sleep deprivation and grief.

Mallika helped me downstairs and put me on the couch, pillows behind me and a warm blanket on top.

"I'll be right back," she said and went into Kara's room.

My thoughts were jumbled. Images from the dream mixed with my own view of Kara's body. They were most vivid when my eyes were closed, so I kept them open, staring at the large stones that made up the fireplace, counting them over and over again. It was only a delaying tactic to avoid thinking about Kara and Eric, but for a while it worked.

When Mallika came back, I knew it was time to confront reality. I sucked in a deep breath and slowly let it out, using some of the meditation techniques Shing had taught me.

Mallika sat beside me, moving the pillows so that my head lay in her lap. It made me feel like a small child, but at that moment I didn't mind. It was comforting, and I needed that more than pride.

"How did you know?" she asked.

I told her about the images that had woken me in the night.

Mallika reached out a hand and stroked my hair. "I see no cause of death for her. Do you think she died because Eric is dead?"

I nodded. This was exactly what I hadn't wanted to think about – the awful reality that I knew Eric was dead, too.

"But why?" I asked. "Why did I see it?"

Mallika looked thoughtful. "I don't know," she said, still stroking my hair. "You are uncharted territory, I'm afraid." But something about the look on her face made me think she wasn't telling me the complete truth.

I wanted to ask more questions, but my eyelids felt too heavy. With each passing second it became harder to think. Between the late hour – what was it, three in the morning? – and the shock of seeing Kara's corpse, my body shut down, and I drifted to sleep.

***

I awoke on the couch alone, light streaming in through the windows. How long had I slept?

I forced myself off the couch and stumbled around the house until I found Mallika sitting in the kitchen, clutching a cup of tea. Her eyes were bloodshot, her face streaked with tears. I felt guilty for falling asleep and leaving her to grieve by herself.

"Oh Mallika, I'm so sorry," I said.

She gave me a wan, tired smile. "Don't be, child. None of this was your fault."

Without warning the tears came. Mallika's words had opened a door in my thoughts that I had desperately tried to keep closed.

It was my fault. Kara and Eric were dead because of me.

If it weren't for me, none of this would have happened. I rejected him and was careless enough to let him see me kissing Rhys. I was sure that's what put him over the edge and ultimately led to his death.

Mallika stood up and pulled me into a hug, but the guilt and pain were too much for me to hold in and I cried – loud and gasping sobs. The kind of tears that come when you know things will never be okay again.

"I know this isn't the right time for this," said Mallika, "but I don't think there ever will be a 'right' time and it's something you need to know."

"What is it?"

"I got a call from Shing while you were asleep," she said. "You were right, Eric is dead."

There it was. My worst fear confirmed.

"How did he die?" I asked, but I was afraid I already knew the answer.

"Osadyn killed him," Mallika said. "He spilled Eric's lifeblood on Margil's seal and freed him."

Spilled Eric's lifeblood.

The words seemed woefully inadequate to describe what must have happened – a euphemism to make his horrible slaughter sound less disturbing.

My mind assaulted me with unwanted images of that moment. I saw Osadyn dangling Eric's limp body from a taloned hand. His throat slit. Blood splattering on the floor. The seal dissolving and a monstrous figure starting to emerge.

I felt nauseated. Sick. Like I would never feel good again. If I hadn't already thrown up earlier, I would have given serious consideration to doing so again.

Instead, I began shaking uncontrollably and dropped to the ground in a gradual collapse.

Mallika helped me back to the couch. Having determined that I needed to be in my own bed, but that I was in no shape to drive home, she picked up the phone and called my dad to pick me up. I tried to protest, but it was too late.

***

Neither my dad nor I spoke on the trip home. The memory of our fight about Rhys a barrier between us that neither of us was willing to knock down.

I sequestered myself in my room for the next two days, hardly eating or drinking anything. Why should I bother? I didn't deserve to be happy. Eric and Kara's deaths were on my conscience, and I would live with that burden for the rest of my life.

Eventually, I reached some sort of crying threshold and the tears stopped. I was spent, exhausted, and utterly unable to sleep. My head felt too full – it couldn't possibly hold that many thoughts and emotions at once.

My parents knocked on the door several times per day, wondering how I was doing. I ignored them and lay on the bed staring at the ceiling, trying not to think about anything.

After I'd spent two solid days in my room, Mom came in and insisted that I come downstairs for lunch. I had no appetite, but she was stubborn and practically dragged me down the stairs.

As I walked past a mirror I saw just how terrible I looked. My face was puffy, my hair a tangled, matted mess, and my eyes looked dull and vacant. Intellectually, I could see that I was a wreck, but emotionally I couldn't bring myself to care.

Mom sat me at the kitchen table and put a bowl of chicken noodle soup in front of me. If she had been hoping that my hunger would compel me to eat, she was disappointed. In fact, the smell of the food made me feel nauseated, and I pushed the bowl away.

"Madison," Mom said, putting her hand on mine. "I'm sorry this happened. I know how tough it is when people you care about die. But, honey, you need to eat. You're scaring us."

I didn't eat.

Mom's next tactic was to move me to the living room, rather than upstairs in my bedroom. She began bringing me personal items that she knew were special to me. A necklace from my grandmother, an autographed copy of Alana, by Tamora Pierce, and a small teddy bear Amy had given me back when we were in junior high.

None of them elicited any reaction from me. But when she

brought me the wooden box that held the spoon Rhys had carved, the fog thinned slightly. I reached out for the box, gently setting it in my lap. I undid the clasp and pulled out the spoon, feeling the smooth wood between my fingers and tracing the outlines of the carved, intertwined hearts on the handle.

"Rhys," I said. My voice was low and rough. It was the first word I had spoken in days. Just saying his name triggered an almost physical reaction, an ache to be with him, to be held in his arms.

From that moment on, I held onto the spoon with a super death grip and refused to put it down. It was a bright hope, holding off the despair that surrounded me. When I held it and thought of Rhys, I could envision an end to this sadness that threatened to drown me.

On the fourth day after Kara and Eric had died, Rhys came to see me. I heard the doorbell ring, but I was too detached from my surroundings to care. However, my dad's raised voice caught my attention.

"Go away," Dad said. "How dare you come here? You're forbidden to see my daughter."

Forbidden. There was that word again. For the first time in days, I felt something other than crushing sadness – irritation.

"I don't want to fight, Scottie," said Rhys' voice, and it was the sweetest sound I had ever heard. "I need to see Madison. She needs me."

"You are the last thing she needs right now." Dad's voice rose, and I could hear the anger and betrayal in it. "She was perfectly fine before she got involved with you."

Clutching the spoon, I crossed through the kitchen into the entryway where Dad and Rhys were facing off in a showdown about to get epic. Dad stood with his back to me, blocking the hallway so Rhys couldn't get through. Rhys looked ready to shove his way past.

"Rhys," I said, savoring the feel of his name.

Rhys' eyes flicked up, locking with mine. His hard expression seemed to melt as he saw me, and I saw my own pain reflected in him.

I held up my hand clutching the spoon, like a talisman to ward off evil. I opened my arms and Rhys pushed past my dad sweeping me up in a powerful embrace.

A dam seemed to break inside of me. All the sadness and pain I had been bottling up since Kara's death broke forth in a tidal wave of emotions. Tears that I thought had dried up streamed down my face, only this time they were accompanied by a cleansing, healing sensation.

"I came as soon as I could," said Rhys. "We had to... clean up."

"I know." I hugged him tighter. I never wanted to let him go.

For the next few minutes we stayed there, locked in an embrace, my face pressed against his chest. I held him tight, my arms refusing to let go now that they had found something solid to grasp. For the first time in days, the overwhelming tide of despair that had threatened to drown my soul began to recede. I could still feel the pain, but I could envision a time when I might be happy again.

When we finally let go of one another, Dad was no longer there. We found him sitting at the kitchen table, staring at his hands, clasping and unclasping them.

We stood in the entryway, holding hands, neither of us sure what to expect.

Dad stood up and walked to me, his expression unreadable. He gently took my head in his hands, the way he had when I was a little girl and he wanted to make sure neither of us were distracted by our surroundings.

"Do you really love him?" he asked.

I nodded. "More than I can ever explain."

Rhys squeezed my hand.

"Are you sure you know what you are getting into?" he asked. "You realize that he is not a seventeen-year-old boy, but a hundred-and-eighty-year-old man?"

"Believe me, Dad," I said. "Every argument as to why this will be difficult has been spelled out for me very clearly. Rhys was very stubborn."

Dad raised an eyebrow. "Rhys told you why you shouldn't be together?"

"Frequently, and in a multitude of ways," I said. "But in the end there was one reason why we should be together that triumphed over the reasons we should be apart."

"And what was that?"

I shrugged and held up the hand holding the love spoon. "I didn't want to give back this cool spoon."

Rhys snorted and the mingled look of shock and amusement on Dad's face was unbelievably satisfying. After a moment, he gave a weak chuckle and held out his hand.

"May I see it?"

I handed him the spoon, and he ran his fingers over it, examining every inch. When he was through he handed it back and addressed Rhys.

"I know what that means to you to. I hadn't realized you felt that strongly about Madison." He took a deep breath and let it out. I could almost see a physical transformation as his expression softened back into the Dad I knew and loved.

He took my hand and held it for a moment. "I still think you're rushing into this, but I do remember what it was like to fall in love. It's obvious that if I want to be a part of your life, this is something I'll have to accept."

I threw my arms around my dad and stood on tip toes to give him my hardest non-'zerking hug.

When I let go, Dad's eyes were bright. He shook his head. "I knew this day would come eventually. I just didn't think it would be this soon."

I rolled my eyes. "Let's not get all dramatic. It's not like I'm going anywhere."

"I know," Dad said with a shrug. "It's a parent thing. One day when you have kids you'll understand."

"Are we okay now?" Rhys asked my dad, motioning between the two of them.

Reaching out, Dad pulled Rhys into one of those loud man-hugs with lots of slapping each other on the back. They always looked painful to me but for some reason guys seemed to like them.

"We're fine," Dad said.

"Good. Then may I stay here and take care of your daughter?"

Dad looked at me and raised an eyebrow. "Going off of past experience, I'm guessing Madison might want to go get cleaned up first."

I suddenly realized what I must look like. I had been too excited to see Rhys, too determined to make Dad accept our relationship to remember that I had hardly been off the couch in two days and hadn't bathed for at least four. I reached up and felt my matted, tangled mess of hair, a flush of embarrassment rushing over me.

I 'zerked, letting the bright glow obscure the more horrible details. "I'll be right back," I said and ran up the stairs to the bathroom in record time.

***

The next day Rhys and Mallika questioned me about the night Eric and Kara had died. I did my best to explain how I'd known something was wrong, but it was hard to explain that suffocating rush of images. Rhys seemed genuinely perplexed, but the expression on Mallika's face and the questions she asked me made me wonder if she knew more than she was telling.

A dark shadow of solemnity seemed to cover the remaining Berserkers. Some took it better than others. Shing remained his usual stoic self, and aside from an extra dose of seriousness, Davu, Arthur, and Josiah, seemed unaffected by the tragedy.

Aata, however, was a complete mess. He and Kara had never made up, and the guilt was eating him alive. He attempted to drink himself into a stupor, but apparently his Berserker-enhanced liver made it impossible. So he took to going out on his own to remote areas and, well, going berserk. It was a strange coping mechanism, but it seemed to work. He always came back looking calmer, but the effect only lasted a day or so before he had to go out again.

We all hoped this wasn't the beginning of a second Berserker going feral.

I was still affected by what had happened, and I suspected on some level I always would be. Eric and Kara were my friends and to have them gone so quickly just seemed wrong somehow - like I had been cheated out of my fair share of time with them.

Fortunately, now that my initial shock was past, I was able to cope and move on with my life. Mom and Dad seemed very relieved to have a daughter who spoke and bathed on a daily basis.

Going back to school was difficult. We couldn't tell anyone about what happened to Eric, so I was expected to be my usual chipper self. Ok, that might be pushing it a bit, but I was expected to act somewhat normal.

During my absence – I told everyone I had gotten food poisoning – Amy and Ginger had engaged in an epic battle of manipulation and spite, but I honestly didn't care anymore. I listened attentively for Amy's sake, but it was hard to concentrate on the complicated battle plans for her next preemptive attack.

When I accidentally let my feelings about it slip to Amy during gym class, she got rather upset and wouldn't talk to me for the rest of the day.

That night after Berserker training – my first training session in weeks – Rhys and I went onto the back porch to cool off.

The night was cooler than usual and there were no clouds. The stars were out, and we sat together on the porch swing looking at the night sky.

After a few moments, Rhys reached under the cushion on the swing. He pulled out a flat package wrapped with a silver ribbon.

"I want you to have this," he said.

"What is it?"

"Open it and find out."

I carefully untied the ribbon and removed the silky red cloth. Underneath was a book beautifully bound in black leather with patterns of sliver leaves and vines twining around the edges. The cover had an image of two masks, one smiling and the other frowning – the classic symbols of comedy and tragedy.

I traced my fingers over the artwork. "It's beautiful."

"Open it up."

I opened the book, and on the first page was a quote from Shakespeare's As You Like It: "All the world's a stage, And all the men and women merely players; They have their exits and their entrances; And one man in his time plays many parts..."

The rest of the book was filled with photos of things Rhys and I had done together: the forest where we first met, the skating rink,

Cannon Beach, Powell's books, Goblin Valley, and dozens of others. Each photo was captioned in neat script explaining why it was significant. There were several pages capturing memories of the play with photos I had no idea he had taken.

"This is beautiful," I said. I reached out and squeezed his hand.

"You like it, then?" Rhys had a shy look on his face, as if he thought I might reject it.

"Of course," I said. "It might be the most thoughtful gift anyone has ever given me."

I continued flipping through the pages. About halfway through the book the pictures ended, leaving blank pages. But the last page with anything on it had simply a date and time: May 2nd, 7:00. That was a little over two weeks from now.

"What's this for?"

"For what I hope will be our next big memory together," Rhys said. "I know it's late notice, but I would be honored if you would go to the Prom with me."

I seemed to be cursed to have good things happen at the wrong times. I had been looking forward to this moment ever since Rhys and I had started dating, but given everything that had happened, it somehow felt... wrong to go to Prom.

I shut the book and closed my eyes. This would be hard enough without having to see the pain I was going to cause him. "I'm sorry, but I can't."

There was a long pause before Rhys answered. "I must admit that wasn't the answer I was hoping for."

I opened my eyes. "I know. I'm sorry, I really do want to go. It's just that given what happened to Eric and Kara, I'm just not ready to go out and party."

"Okay," said Rhys. "I understand and can respect that. But may I give you an alternate perspective before you make a final decision?"

"Sure."

Rhys held up a hand and counted the reasons off as he spoke. "First, staying home will not bring either Eric or Kara back. Second, both Eric and Kara would have wanted you to do what made you happy. Third, the last thing you need right now is to be dwelling on something that was not your fault and was completely out of your control. And fourth, all the preparations for Prom will keep you occupied while you come to terms with their deaths."

I took in a deep breath before answering. "Logically I understand, and it makes sense," I said.

"So you'll come?"

I shook my head. "I guess I'm just not a logical person, because it still doesn't feel right to go."

"It doesn't feel right?"

"Yeah, it somehow feels... disrespectful to be going out and having fun so quickly after they died."

"So how long will you have to punish yourself before you're allowed to have fun again?" He looked me straight in the eyes. Oh those eyes!

"Rhys," I said. "It's not like that." Or was it? Hadn't he hit the nail on the head? Wasn't that what I was doing? They had suffered and so

I should too?

"Believe me," he said. "I understand the feeling. It took me a lot of years after I faked my own death to feel like I was allowed to have fun. Don't make the same mistake I did. Punishing yourself for something that isn't your fault only leads to more pain."

"I know."

"Besides, you and I both know that Eric would never want anyone, anywhere, at anytime to miss a party because of him."

I let out a laugh. That was true. No one loved to have fun more than Eric.

"I don't know," I said.

Rhys reached out and held my hand. "If I thought that by staying home you would get through this faster, I wouldn't even have asked. But from what I have seen, the only way to get through these kinds of trials is to keep yourself immersed in life. Life heals."

I leaned over and wrapped my arms around Rhys' neck. I gently pressed my lips to his – they were amazingly soft – and then pulled back.

"Have I ever told you that you are a wise man?"

Rhys smiled and kissed me again. "Is that a yes?"

***

Amy was so excited to hear I was going to Prom with Rhys that she forgot she was mad at me. We spent the next few days looking around for a Prom dress, and after hours of searching, finally found the perfect one. The choices had been slim since I was getting into this rather late, but when I saw the dress, it was like a chorus of angels was singing, and light shone down on it from above.

The satin dress was lavender and flowed down to the floor with a gathered waist, beaded appliqué, and capped sleeves. When I tried it on, it fit as perfectly as if it had been tailor made for me. It was elegant and beautiful.

"Wow," said Amy when I tried it on. "I am so dancing on the other side of the room from you."

I looked down at the dress, confused by her comment. "Why, don't you like it?"

"Oh, I like it, all right," she said. "It's gorgeous. That's the problem. I'm going to feel like a dandelion next to an orchid."

***

Two nights before Prom I was awakened by the sensation that something was horribly wrong.

I sat bolt upright up in bed, adrenaline causing me to pre-zerk. There were no lights on in the room, but with my heightened senses, I could see clearly. I scanned the room, but nothing seemed to be out of the ordinary.

So what had woke me up?

And then I felt it – that strange sixth sense that told me when creatures of darkness were nearby. It was strong and... different somehow. Not strong enough to be Osadyn, but too strong for

Bringers. Unless there was an army of them.

That thought was all it took to transition me into a full 'zerk.

I grabbed my varé off my dresser and dashed to the window, throwing it open, my eyes scouring the trees for any sign of attack.

I saw nothing.

The feeling of darkness grew stronger, causing waves of nausea to wash over me. Whatever was causing this feeling wasn't here yet, but it was coming closer.

I leaped from the window and effortlessly dropped to the ground. I flicked open my varé and stood in a defensive posture. I would not be taken by surprise.

A rustle in the bushes caused me to spin around in time to see Eric walking out of the shadows.

"Madison!" he said, his arms held out wide as if waiting for me to rush in for a hug. "I was just coming to see you."

I took a step back. This couldn't be right – Eric was dead.

"What's the matter?" he asked, his arms still outstretched. "You don't look happy to see me."

"You're dead," I said.

Eric dropped his arms to his sides. "That's right," he said. "I am. Does that bother you? Are you prejudiced against the dead? I thought you were more open-minded than that." He gave me a mocking smile.

"What's going on?" I asked. "What are you doing here?"

"Oh, I just thought we had a little unfinished business," Eric said, taking a step towards me. "Since, you know, it's your fault I died and all."

The words stung. It hurt to have him so matter-of-factly articulate my shameful fears – to know that it wasn't just my overly-developed sense of guilt, but that Eric himself blamed me for his death.

"I'm sorry."

"Sorry?" Eric let out a laugh, but something about it was off. It sounded too harsh, like rocks being rubbed together. "Sorry doesn't make it better. Sorry doesn't bring back all those people I killed in Brookings-Harbor. Sorry doesn't take away your guilt or remove their innocent blood from your hands." As he spoke his grin grew wider and wider, until it stretched so far his lips actually split open revealing teeth and gums. There was no blood, just the white of bone and the pink of exposed flesh.

Horrified, I took a step back, anything to keep away from whatever Eric had become.

"Stay away from me," I said, and I was proud to hear that, despite my fear, my voice sounded firm and steady.

"What's the matter? I just want a little kiss." Eric leered, the split skin of his face flopping obscenely. "Come on, you gave it up for Rhys, I just want my turn."

He took another step towards me and I pointed the varé at his chest.

"Keep back."

"What are you going to do? Kill me again? Fine." He pushed forward, impaling himself on the blade. The varé sunk in several inches until it passed completely through his chest and out the back.

"Now can I have my kiss?"

I yanked the varé out of his chest, ripping more of his flesh in the process. He looked down at the gaping hole in his chest, which to my horror was not bleeding at all.

"Of course, this wound pales in comparison to the way you hurt me when you kissed Rhys." He lunged towards me, arms outstretched. I spun out of the way and he ran past me, stumbling to a halt. Whatever had happened to him, he no longer had the quickness or strength of a Berserker.

"What do you want?" I asked.

The flesh along Eric's jaw had continued to rip, and now half of his face was peeling off, exposing white bone and sinew. His eyes rolled up in his head and his voice took on a deeper timbre.

"I want you to feel pain like I did. I want you to know despair and hopelessness. I want to spill your blood and break the seal," he said, and charged me again.

Watching his face flap as he ran put me over the edge. I simply could not deal with it any longer. My conscious mind retreated, and my body reacted on its own. As Eric ran by, I slashed my varé into his side, cutting deeply into his torso and peeling back flesh.

Eric hardly seemed to notice. "This is all your fault, Madison!" he shrieked and charged again. "Why couldn't you have just loved me?"

Once again my Berserker reflexes sent the varé slashing out, this time hitting Eric in the shoulder. The blow nearly severed his arm. It dangled limply at his side, obviously too injured to move. By now half of Eric's face had peeled off and with the other half he glared at me, his expression dominated by an all consuming rage.

"You teased me and led me on," he wailed. "Made me think we had a future together."

This detachment I felt was surreal. My conscious mind that was watching from a hidden corner wanted to scream out a denial, to tell him it had all been a misunderstanding – I had repeatedly told him I wasn't interested. But that would have meant coming out and facing the full force of the mental anguish and pain that awaited me. Part of me must have known that wasn't such a hot idea and pushed my conscious mind even farther away.

Eric reached a hand up and peeled away the remaining half of his face like a horrific Halloween mask, carelessly throwing it to the ground. His head was now a monstrosity. Bits of muscle and tendon still clung to his skull, and his eyes rolled wildly in their sockets.

"Now I will sacrifice you and free the others!" Eric raised his one good arm, his hand outstretched to claw me. He charged, a deranged half-dead nightmare come to life.

And that was when my mind decided it had had enough.

***

My next memory was hearing my dad calling my name.

"Madison? Madison?"

Strong arms reached around me and tried to push my arms down to my side. But my arms didn't want to stop. They wanted to continue hacking with the varé.

"Madison, honey, you need to put the varé down."

And then I was back. My conscious mind returned to control, and I stopped hacking at the pile of shredded flesh and shattered bones on the grass. Numbly, I let the varé slip from my fingers and tumble to the ground.

"Dad?" I asked. How had he gotten here? How had I gotten here? My thoughts were all confused.

"It's me, Madison," he said. He turned me to face him, away from the carnage at my feet.

I felt hot tears streaming down my face. The memories came rushing back – a horror movie come to life and played out in my yard.

I tried to explain what had happened, but the words wouldn't come – they were constantly interrupted by wracking sobs.

"Let's get you cleaned up," Dad said. He took me inside, and while I showered he disposed of my carnage covered pajamas. As the hot water poured over me, I scrubbed my skin until it was raw, but no matter how much I washed, I still felt filthy on the inside.

I couldn't get Eric's words out of my mind. I'd already half believed the accusations that were now burned into my thoughts. And I had just killed him again. Not just killed him, but psycho-serial-killer chopped him up. What was wrong with me?

I put on some fresh pajamas and went downstairs. Sleep was an impossibility now. Even if I could have slept, I didn't want to face the dreams that surely awaited me.

Dad sat with me on the couch, tucking my head against his

shoulder and holding my hand like he had when I had fallen off my bike as a child. He tried to talk with me, but I couldn't bring myself to engage in conversation.

After a while Dad got up and left me alone on the couch wrapped up in a blanket, doing my best to keep my mind blank and to pretend tonight had never happened.

A few minutes later, the front door opened without anyone knocking. Rhys strode into the living room, his eyes concerned, his expression determined. He stopped when he saw me on the couch, and his features softened.

He started to lower himself to the floor near me, but I was already off the couch, throwing my arms around him.

The night's events tumbled out of me, a veritable flood of words. "I killed him," I said, when I was done. "I killed him."

"No you didn't," said Rhys, squeezing me tight. "Don't you dare blame yourself for this."

"Who do I blame, then?" The words were thick and barely half-enunciated.

"Margil," said a voice from the entrance to the living room. I pulled my gaze away from Rhys as Dad walked in. He reached out a hand and stroked the back of my head.

"I don't understand."

"Margil's power," said Rhys, "is over dead things. Just as Osadyn can control emotions, Margil has control over the dead. He can reanimate a corpse or accelerate decay.

"Eric was already dead. What made him Eric had fled long ago.

What you saw was Eric's reanimated corpse, controlled by Margil."

"But-"

"He was dead, Madison," said Dad. "Why do you think there was no blood when you stabbed him? Osadyn had already drained it to break the seal and free Margil. That wasn't Eric you killed, it was Margil's power wearing Eric's already dead body."

I wanted to believe it wasn't Eric. I wanted to believe that he had never said those horrible things to me, but it was difficult. "It was him. He knew things that Margil could never know."

"No," said Rhys. He pulled me over to the couch and sat me down. He knelt in front of me, holding my hand and looking at me with such a troubled expression that I almost felt I should be the one comforting him. "We know Eric died," Rhys said. "The seal was broken and Margil was freed. That could not happen unless Eric died. Kara died without a physical cause. That wouldn't have happened unless her Berserker died."

I turned toward my dad, who was looking up at the ceiling. He knew firsthand what happened to a Binder when her Berserker died.

"There is nothing to doubt in this," Rhys continued. "I am one hundred percent sure he is dead. When Margil reanimated Eric's body, he gained access to some of Eric's stronger memories. That's all."

I wiped the tears from my eyes and nodded. "I guess that makes sense," I said. "It just felt so real."

Rhys got off his knees and sat on the couch next to me. He put his arm around me, and I rested my head on his shoulder.

"I know," he said. "That's what Margil wanted you to think. These monsters will do anything to gain an advantage. Believe me, this isn't the worst thing they've tried."

I was tempted to ask what the worst thing was, but my eyes were already burning, and I was having a hard time staying awake. I didn't want to sleep, but if Rhys was here, I would give it a try.

"Don't leave me," I said.

Rhys lifted a hand and gently caressed my cheek. "I won't."

With that I closed my eyes and fell asleep.

CHAPTER 12

WORST. PROM. EVER.

The day of the Prom, Mom took me out to get a full makeover – hairstyling, manicure, makeup – the works. Prom had been a defining moment for her, and she was determined to inflict that experience on me.

After what had happened with Eric, I'd tried to back out of going, but Mom did everything in her power to convince me to still go.

Mom had the haze on her, so she didn't fully understand what was happening, but she did understand that some close friends had died and that I was grieving for them.

"You need to go," she said. "Prom is practically a rite of passage."

I tried to argue, but she and Rhys teamed up on me until I finally consented. I really did want to go, just not like this. Not with Eric's words echoing in my head, his accusations vivid in my memory.

But that evening when I saw myself in the mirror after everything was done, I understood why Mom was so insistent. It was the first time in my life that everything had come together at once – hair, makeup, nails, and clothes. For the first time in my life I actually felt beautiful. I was no longer awkward preteen Madison, nor was I Berserker Madison who spent her evenings training to kill monsters. It was like living in some alternate reality where for one evening I was a model or – I was embarrassed even to think it – a princess. I even had a matching purse to go with the dress. It wasn't very big so I had to make some strategic choices about what to bring. In the end I opted for a small container of lip gloss, my EpiPen, and the varé. After what had happened with Eric, I wasn't going to go anywhere unarmed again.

When Rhys showed up wearing an expensively cut black tux, the expression on his face was difficult to decipher. He said nothing and just stared at me, looking slightly confused.

I shifted uncomfortably and smoothed the front of my dress. "Do I look ok?" I asked, suddenly feeling insecure.

My question startled Rhys out of his thoughts. He gave me a smile that made all my time spent in preparation worth it. "You are dazzling," he said. "Easily the most beautiful woman I have seen in well over a hundred years."

That would do.

* * *

Rhys had agreed to keep our Prom night simple. No renting out an entire restaurant or going anywhere on a chartered jet – just a quiet dinner and then straight to Prom.

Instead of the usual Range Rover, Rhys had come in a two-seater BMW convertible he had bought for the occasion. Not exactly in the spirit of our agreement, but not technically against it either, as Rhys pointed out, since I had only told him not to rent a limo and never mentioned anything about purchasing a new car.

He drove us down to Portland for dinner in a restaurant on top of one of the tallest buildings in the city. The food was amazing and the view of the sunset was spectacular. We talked and laughed. Gradually my reluctance faded in the face of such a wonderful evening.

About halfway through dinner, Rhys' cell phone vibrated. He checked the number and sighed.

"It's Aata," he said. "He knows what tonight is and wouldn't call me unless it was really important. Do you mind?"

"Go ahead," I said.

He walked out of the main dining area so he wouldn't disturb the other guests. When he returned five minutes later, his face was grim.

"What happened?"

Rhys sat back down and scooted his chair in. "They found a temperature spike out at the coast. They're going to check it out."

"Do we need to go?" I asked.

"No. It's probably nothing. And if it isn't, they can take care of it themselves."

"Are you sure?"

"I'm sure. This is your special night and I don't want anything to ruin it. Besides, it's probably nothing."

I heard the words he said, but the expression on his face told a very different story.

***

After dinner, we drove to the hotel where Prom was being held. Amy had been on the committee and was in charge of decorations. Like everything she did, she went as over the top as possible. To enter into the dance, we had to walk through a tunnel of lights. The main ballroom had been covered from floor to ceiling in lights, to look like stars and the moon. Dozens of round tables with lacy white table cloths outlined the dance floor. From the main chandelier, hundreds of strands of lights streamed out across the ceiling.

Before I could finish taking everything in, Amy spotted us and ran over squealing with delight.

"You're here! I'm so glad you made it!" She stopped and held me at arm's-length, looking me up and down. "Curse you and your regal good looks! You're every bit as beautiful as I was afraid you'd be. Now I must destroy you." She pulled me in and gave me a tight embrace.

"Speaking of beautiful," I said. "The decorations look almost as good as you."

Amy gave me a shy smile, and then burst out laughing. "Yeah, they turned out all right, didn't they?" Before we could talk more, one of the other girls on the decorating committee pulled her away to deal with some emergency.

The dance floor was packed with kids swaying – with varying

degrees of success – to the music. I had never been a great dancer, but I wasn't bad. Add in my Berserker-enhanced coordination and balance, and I was actually pretty good now. I didn't know very many moves, but once I'd seen a move done by someone else, I could easily replicate it.

We had only been dancing for a few minutes when Selma Torres came up to me, dragging Mason Cross behind her. She was wearing a lilac dress with spaghetti straps and a ruffled skirt.

"Madison!" she yelled with far too much enthusiasm. If her excessive exuberance hadn't given her away, I would have been able to tell by the smell that she had been drinking. She let go of Mason's hand and gave me a big hug. "You look so beautiful!"

"Thanks!" I said. "I love your dress."

"Thanks! You're so sweet. We really should hang together more next year," she said. She hadn't let go of the hug and was now practically hanging on me.

"Okay," I said, trying to extract myself from this awkward embrace. "That sounds like a great idea." I wondered if she would remember this conversation in the morning.

For the next hour, I was assailed by wave after wave of girls telling me how beautiful I looked. It was really strange. Some of them were drunk like Selma and expressed their profound regret that we hadn't spent more time together. But others were just acquaintances who – under some mysterious Prom-night spell – wanted to compliment me.

Amy came by and danced with us for a bit, but it was extremely awkward. Josh tagged along obediently, but stayed off to the side and wouldn't meet my eyes. Fortunately, Amy was in a social mood and didn't stay in any one place for very long.

A couple of times I caught sight of Ginger Johnson's red hair, but the dance floor was so packed that I never got a good look at her. We hadn't really spoken since the day she'd told me she would keep my secret. We certainly weren't friends, but surprisingly she had kept her word, and as an added bonus she hadn't made my life miserable for the rest of the year.

One of the benefits of being a Berserker was that I could dance for hours without a break. As the night went on, other people started getting sweaty and rumpled, but Rhys and I were as dry as we had been when we started dancing.

But it was getting hot.

My head started pounding, and I felt a little nauseated. Something I had eaten at dinner must not have agreed with me.

"Let's sit down," I told Rhys. "I think I need a bit of a break."

We walked back to the table where we had left our things. My nausea grew, and just a few steps from the chair, I felt shooting pains go through my head. My knees buckled. Fortunately, Rhys caught me before I completely embarrassed myself by collapsing on the floor.

"What's wrong?" he asked, helping me to a chair.

By this time my head was pounding with a killer headache. It felt like someone was inside my skull banging around with a sledge hammer.

"Head hurts," was all I managed to get out before I was assaulted by a flood of images.

- Tattooed warriors making grotesque faces.

- A small boy wearing only a pair of dirty shorts.

- A sandy beach under a clear blue sky.

- Snow covered mountains.

- A tiny German village.

- Playing in a soccer match.

- Begging for food on the street.

The pain in my head exploded, my skull feeling as if it had shattered. Heat and nausea rolled over me in thick waves, blocking out everything else as I tried not to throw up. Not here. Not tonight.

A violent vibration shook the room. Screams erupted all around me. I looked up to see people running in all directions, scrambling for the exits.

"Earthquake!" Someone yelled, followed by dozens of less-coherent screams.

Another vibration hit, knocking over the DJ's speakers, toppling tables, and sending streamers collapsing to the floor.

And then through the distraction of my headache, the nausea, and the pounding walls, I felt a darkness I had only experienced a handful of times before.

A Havoc was near.

I looked up to see Rhys already on his feet, his varé in hand, but not yet unrolled.

By now only a few people were left in the room, which was good because at that moment, the south wall exploded inward, sending brick, wood, and plaster everywhere.

A new wave of nausea and heat flooded over me, and this time I was unable to resist vomiting my dinner all over the floor.

When I looked up, the entire wall was gone. In its place stood Osadyn, surrounded by several dozen Bringers. The Bringers streamed into the room, flowing around Osadyn like a nasty grey tidal wave of slime.

We 'zerked and pulled out our varés. I flicked mine open and felt the familiar extension of my arm.

My 'zerking didn't usually have the same component of rage that the other Berserkers felt, but this time anger flooded through me. Osadyn had attacked my Prom and put my friends in danger.

I rushed to the oncoming Bringers and hacked through two of them with my first slash. I tried a backhand cut at a third, but my dress tangled up my feet, and I had to change direction at the last second or trip.

Ultimately life is about choices, and in that moment I had to choose between my beautiful, perfect dress and staying alive. Which wasn't much of a choice at all, but it did make me sick to think about what I had to do.

The varé sliced through the material easily and in the space of a few heartbeats my dress was significantly shorter. Unfortunately, that was enough of a distraction to allow a Bringer to wrap its arms around me and unhinge its jaws.

I struggled to get free, but two more Bringers joined the first, and my arms were pinned to my side with no leverage to break out.

Desperate, I flung myself forwards, pitching to the ground. The impact dislodged one of the Bringers, giving me enough space to fling my arms apart and escape.

I jumped to my feet, and in three strokes I had cut the Bringers into quickly dissolving piles of goo. There was no time to celebrate or even make witty remarks, so I turned my attention to the next wave of Bringers pouring through the ravaged wall.

I fought my way over to Rhys' side. We had trained for just such an occasion, and by now each of us knew instinctively what the other was going to do.

Together we swung our varés, killing the Bringers in an elegant – if extremely gruesome – dance. There was a rhythm to it that we both felt, and together we literally cut our way across the dance floor toward Osadyn.

As we approached the Havoc, I felt the temperature around me spiking and my nausea increasing. Dancing may not have taxed our stamina, but between the heat of Osadyn and the exertion of killing all those Bringers, I could feel sweat pouring off of me now.

Osadyn reared on two legs, wildly flailing its front feet. Its long neck whipped around frantically and then stiffened, pointing directly at us.

Immediately I felt a sense of calm and peace surrounding me. Why was I fighting? Everything was going to be all right. It would be much easier to simply sit down and rest.

I rejected this thought as soon as it came. Everything was not going to be all right. We needed to stop Osadyn and do it now.

To my left I saw Rhys slow to a stop, the glow of his 'zerk starting to flicker. What was going on?

"Not real," said Rhys. His words were barely audible; his expression peaceful.

And then I realized what was happening. Osadyn was manipulating our emotions, but this time, instead of projecting fear and anger, it was creating a feeling of peace and calm to stop the adrenalin that triggered our 'zerking.

After a moment, Rhys' glow disappeared completely. The two dozen remaining Bringers rushed forward and pinned him to the ground. Through the flailing limbs of the Bringers, I saw his eyes open, staring at me intently – trying to communicate. He mouthed a single word – "go".

I should have been horrified at the scene before me. Intellectually, I knew that my feelings should be ones of revulsion, fear, and anger, but I could feel none of that. Instead, a feeling of overwhelming happiness colored my thoughts, dominating my emotions and overlaying them with something utterly artificial – a bucket of neon pink paint being dumped on the Mona Lisa.

Slowly, I felt my heart rate drop, and the glow surrounding me disappeared. Without adrenaline to trigger our powers, Rhys and I were helpless. We still retained our natural Berserker defenses, but we lacked the power to attack or escape.

I became so relaxed that my body couldn't remain standing. I collapsed to the ground, my varé falling uselessly from my fingers.

I watched helplessly as Osadyn lumbered toward Rhys. For the moment Osadyn seemed to have no interest in me. It was Rhys' blood that could bind Osadyn, and it had every reason to want him dead.

Held down by a dozen Bringers, Rhys fought in vain to 'zerk and free himself, but the emotional effect Osadyn projected was too strong. Even with the threat of impending death approaching, neither Rhys nor I was able to 'zerk.

With a single claw on its front foot, Osadyn pierced the thick muscle of Rhys' shoulder. It was bone, and living bone at that – a very potent weapon against a powerless Berserker.

For a moment, I saw a flash, a brief flicker of a 'zerk surrounding Rhys, and then it was gone. Not even pain could break through to let him 'zerk.

I wanted to cry, to be sad or upset. This eerie sense of wellbeing felt out of place. The disconnect between what I thought and what I felt was overwhelming. My mind tried to rationalize the discrepancy – I saw Rhys in pain, and I felt good, therefore I must not like Rhys. It took enormous concentration not to believe it.

Osadyn took a second claw and drove it completely through Rhys' thigh, pinning him to the ground. He cried out in agony, his 'zerk flickering to life for an instant before once again disappearing.

There was nothing I could do. My mind was too numb and my body too relaxed to even stand up, let alone fight. I was completely helpless, while Osadyn took his time killing Rhys.

Out of the corner of my eye, I saw two figures moving behind an overturned table. Someone else was here. I caught another glance, and this time the red hair was unmistakable – Ginger. And she seemed to be arguing with someone.

Was that Josh?

What could they possibly be thinking? Why hadn't they run out like the rest of the kids?

And then it happened.

Pain flashed through my head like a burst of lightning in a night sky. More pictures, more images.

- A little girl eating fruit from a wooden bowl.

- An elderly man clapping his hands to the rhythm of a song.

- A Berserker running through the night.

- Rhys carrying Mallika to meet me when I had first fought Osadyn.

- Mallika and I embracing, mourning the death of Kara.

There were dozens of images – hundreds even – flashing through my mind so quickly that I couldn't possibly process them all.

And with it all, I felt a thousand different emotions pushing against the web of false peace Osadyn had imposed on me. One by one the strands broke until I felt a wonderful surge of adrenaline coursing through my veins. I 'zerked and leapt to my feet, grabbing my varé.

I ran towards Osadyn pushing my muscles as hard as I could. I leapt onto its back and plunged my varé downward, piercing the hard carapace with a loud crunch and sinking it in to the hilt. Golden fluid spurted from the wound.

Osadyn howled and reared back onto his hind legs, throwing me off. I tried to pull out my varé as I fell, but the monster's blood made the hilt too slippery. My fingers slid off the hilt, leaving the varé still lodged inside him. I hit the floor and slid across it, scattering a table and several chairs. As soon as I stopped, I leapt to my feet for a second attack.

But it wasn't that easy.

Osadyn turned to face me, and I was bombarded with a new wave of emotions – peace, contentment, serenity – only much stronger than before. The massive beast swung its head away from Rhys and peered directly at me with those malevolent eyes. I managed to take a staggering step before once again dropping to my knees. My 'zerk faded under the onslaught of emotions. The images flashing through my mind were no longer strong enough to fuel my 'zerk.

Once my 'zerk faded, Osadyn turned his attention back to Rhys. He lifted another claw into the air, and I saw Rhys shudder as the claw pierced the muscle of his other shoulder. Despite the emotional dampening of Osadyn, on some level it still hurt to see Rhys in pain.

Desperate to help, I tried to use my Binder powers to send out a snare to trap Osadyn. I reached within myself to tap into that power, but all that came out was a thin trickle of black ooze from my fingertips – nothing like the cables I had sent out before. Either Binder powers were somehow tied into emotions or I was too drained to create the snare.

A whisper from nearby pulled my attention away from Osadyn and Rhys. "Pssst. Madison."

I looked up to see Ginger kneeling a few feet away from me, her red hair speckled with bits of white plaster from the decimated wall. She looked somehow – different. Instead of her usual scowl of disdain, she had an expression of grim determination. She knelt behind a table, keeping it between her and Osadyn, a tiny purse clutched in one hand. Josh knelt beside her, holding a splintered table leg like a club.

"Go," I said. "This is dangerous. You shouldn't be here."

Ginger shook her head, and the determination in her face sharpened. "That's what he keeps telling me," she said, motioning to Josh. "Sorry, but I'm not leaving you to fight this thing on your own. What can I do to help?"

What could she do? She was a gifted athlete, but she was no match for Osadyn and the Bringers. I knew she was trying to be brave, but there was nothing she could do right now. Maybe I could have her insult me until I got angry enough to 'zerk.

And then the answer hit me.

Weakly I pointed to the table where Rhys and I had sat. "My purse," I said. "I need my purse."

Ginger didn't question my strange request. She nodded brusquely and headed toward the table. She was only a few feet away from the purse when one of the Bringers saw her.

The Bringer emitted a piercing shriek and ran toward Ginger, its slavering mouth open wide. Josh ran forward and placed himself between Ginger and the Bringer, holding the table leg out like a bat. The Bringer hesitated, giving Ginger time to grab my purse and throw it to me. It landed on the floor right next to me before sliding several feet away.

Josh paid the price for his bravery. From the corner of my eye I saw the Bringer knock the table leg away, unhinge its slimy jaws, and begin to swallow Josh whole.

With the last of the strength I had left, I crawled toward my purse, each foot of distance taking far more energy than something as simple as crawling should do.

I heard slurping noises from the side and knew that Josh was now partway down the throat of the Bringer.

At last my fingers clutched the small purse, and I fumbled the zipper open. There it was, my last chance at survival – my EpiPen. I popped it open and with a trembling hand jabbed it into my leg.

Pain rushed through me. An all-consuming fire that burned away all traces of Osadyn's emotional control. What had felt like ropes binding me down, preventing me from 'zerking, burned away like cobwebs before a flame.

Anger. Hatred. Destruction.

My mind was a blur now, and I felt the overwhelming desire to destroy things. The last time I had used the EpiPen, I wasn't prepared for the onslaught of emotions. This time I knew what to expect and was able to hold off the rage... somewhat.

To my left I saw the Bringer swallowing the last of Josh while Ginger futilely beat at it with the table leg. With the last bit of clarity I could muster, I grabbed the Bringer's head and ripped its jaws apart. Chunks of flesh flew through the air, turning to black goo. I drove one hand through the ribcage of the dying Bringer and with my other hand pried open a hole, tearing the Bringer in half. The remaining flesh turned to black goo, leaving Josh visible under a puddle of nastiness.

"Get him out of here," I said to Ginger. "It's not safe." My voice sounded harsh and raspy, as if it were coming from someone else. Josh's eyes widened at my glowing Berserker rage. Ginger grabbed his hand and together they ran from the ballroom, black goo dripping off Josh and leaving a trail behind them.

Once Ginger and Josh were gone, I stopped resisting and allowed the adrenalin-fueled 'zerk to overtake me. Power flowed. There was nothing I couldn't kill right now, no force on earth that could stop me.

I rushed toward Osadyn, crashed into the massive monster, and knocked it flying across the room. I looked down at Rhys' bleeding body, and my anger burned even hotter. With an incoherent growl, I leaped onto Osadyn's back, punching and clawing. I yanked my varé from its back and plunged it back in repeatedly.

Osadyn howled, rearing back onto his hind legs. But this time I was prepared for that tactic and used the hilt of the varé as a handle, maintaining my position while it tried to throw me off.

Golden blood oozed from a dozen wounds, and for the first time ever, I saw Osadyn start to weaken. He collapsed to his knees, his long neck flopping feebly for a moment before going still.

He was done.

I yanked out my varé and jumped off Osadyn to check on Rhys. He pulled himself into a sitting position. I ran to embrace him. The look of terror on his face told me of my mistake an instant too late.

Pain exploded through my leg, and I found myself lifted into the air, clenched in Osadyn's powerful jaws. It whipped me around and flung me high into the air. For a dizzying instant I felt as if I were flying – light-weight and floating – before I began the quick descent back to the ground. I twisted in the air, attempting to land on my feet. I almost managed it. My heels hit first and slipped out from under me, causing me to land awkwardly on one hip. Had I not been a Berserker, a fall like that would have killed me.

No sooner had I landed than Osadyn once again clamped its jaws on my leg. I could feel the flesh tearing, the teeth sinking down to the bone. The pain was intense – blinding. I felt consciousness starting to fade away.

Abruptly Osadyn let go of my leg and roared. I struggled back to full consciousness and saw Rhys, his arms and legs wrapped around Osadyn's neck squeezing with all his Berserker might. He was 'zerking!

"A snare!" Rhys yelled. "Do it now!"

I reached out my hands and pushed. This time black cables flew out of my fingertips, weaving into a net as they covered Osadyn. Rhys leaped off and rolled clear as the snare descended.

Osadyn roared and thrashed about, trying to break through the cables of my snare. I felt the strain on the snare and struggled mentally to keep it from ripping apart. I had not expected how difficult the snare would be to maintain once Osadyn was trapped in it.

The strain was too much for me, and I collapsed to the floor. My mind was buffeted by dueling forces – the pain from my leg; the effort required to keep the snare from breaking; the fury of my adrenalin enhanced 'zerk; and on top of it all the sickly sweet layer of false peace coming from Osadyn. I wasn't sure how much longer I could hold on to the snare and the 'zerk.

Within moments, my rage ebbed, and I could feel myself burning through the adrenalin I'd injected. The EpiPen wasn't a long-term solution, just a jumpstart.

Like a candle guttering out, the glow around me flickered several times and then disappeared.

With my 'zerking extinguished, Osadyn renewed his efforts to break free of the snare. The cables stretched, and my mind felt the pressure on them. A few of them frayed and snapped, but enough of them held to keep Osadyn trapped.

And then I knew what to do.

The idea came to me whole – a knowledge I couldn't possibly possess. It didn't feel like a new thought. It was more like remembering something from deep inside me – something I had known for a long time.

"Rhys," I said. I had intended to yell, but all that came out was a hoarse whisper. I gestured for him to come to me.

Wasting no time, Rhys came to me, and knelt beside me, holding my face in his hands. He gazed at me with such tenderness that it made my heart ache. I longed to reach out and simply hold him for as long as I could. I wanted nothing more than to fall asleep in his arms.

"Can you hold it?" he asked.

"I can, but not for much longer. I need your blood."

Rhys' expression became confused. He started asking questions, but Osadyn roared and strained against the snare. Between the noise and the concentration required to hold the snare, I didn't hear a word he said.

I picked up my varé and grabbed his wrist. With a quick slicing motion, I drew the base of the blade along the muscle in his inner forearm.

Bright red blood flowed from the wound, pouring to the ground much faster than it should. I could feel the power in it calling to me - somehow connected to me - a weapon waiting to be shaped and used. In the faint light of the ballroom, his blood gave off a bright glow as it pooled on the floor.

Osadyn renewed its efforts to escape. It thrashed wildly, desperately afraid of the blood and what I was going to do with it.

More images flooded my mind. I saw the blood as Osadyn did – a dark and evil fluid. There was fear there – fear of this blood and longing for the shedding of mine. It desperately wanted to free Pravicus.

And behind it all I felt something so unexpected that it almost made me lose my concentration – love. Threaded throughout the images Osadyn sent was an overwhelming feeling of love tinged with sadness and a long-frustrated desire to be with Pravicus.

I pushed the thoughts away. Now was not the time to be distracted. Osadyn had proven to be a master at manipulating my emotions. I would not allow it to deceive me.

My decision was made much easier as Osadyn lunged out with its long neck and bit Rhys on the shoulder. The teeth sunk in deep. I heard a click as they hit bone and Rhys screamed in agony.

With hardly a thought except to free Rhys, I kicked Osadyn in the side of the head. Without my 'zerk, the kick was relatively feeble, but it was enough to distract Osadyn. He opened his jaws and turned his head to regard me malevolently.

Once free from the bite, Rhys reached out and wrapped an arm around Osadyn's neck to keep his head still. Between the snare and Rhys' headlock, the creature couldn't reach me.

I looked down at the pool of blood on the floor and with my mind I willed it into the shape I saw in my head and intuitively knew was right. The blood glowed even brighter than before – liquid light that cast fleeting red shadows across the ballroom as it flowed into a circle two feet in diameter. Around the outside edge of the circle ran a two inch thick strip that was thicker than the interior of the circle. It looked vaguely like a wax seal that had been pressed with a large signet.

I reached down and pressed my right hand firmly into the center of the circle of blood. It was cool to the touch and more substantial than I had expected. Where my skin touched it, the blood parted and my hand sunk down leaving a handprint. Streams of energy erupted around the seal like lightning flashing through the air.

When I pulled my hand back, Osadyn began to thrash even more. Several of my snare cables frayed and broke, but I willed the rest to hold. As I approached, Osadyn tried to thrash his neck about, and managed to lift Rhys slightly off the floor, but Rhys shifted positions and was able to keep control of the head.

I held up my hand, the palm and fingers glowing bright red where they had touched the blood. Osadyn renewed his efforts, but even now I could feel him weakening. I pressed the palm of my hand to Osadyn's head, directly between the eyes.

He screamed.

A thousand more images burst through my mind – images of pain, loss, sorrow, and fear. I saw myself as Osadyn saw me, bright and terrible, a being of pain and anguish. I was a hunter, a jailor, an executioner.

Part of me recoiled at the sight of myself through Osadyn's eyes. What kind of horror was I?

But the other part of me recognized that Osadyn was trying to do the same thing to me. He wanted Rhys dead to prevent him from being bound, and he wanted my blood to free Pravicus. I could see from the images he sent that he would never rest until Pravicus was free. It was bind or be killed.

I chose to bind.

With a last great effort I created a mental connection between the handprint in the seal and the handprint on Osadyn.

Slowly, the color drained out of Osadyn and into the seal. As I watched, Osadyn became less substantial, his essence flowing out of its corporeal body.

The seal turned from red to a bright golden color, sending out threads of light too bright to look at. At the same time, Osadyn became an insubstantial outline, drained of all solidity and vibrancy. He was literally a shadow of his former self, insubstantial and unable to interact with anything or even be seen by anyone but Rhys and myself. The light flared brighter, causing me to raise my arm to shield my eyes, and then went out. A dimly glowing golden seal remained on the floor – a golden seal with a red handprint in the center.

Osadyn thrashed, kicking and biting at anything he could reach, but he could no longer interact on this plane of existence and passed harmlessly through the objects he attempted to destroy. He raised his head to howl his frustration and anger, but no sound came out.

Osadyn was bound.

Exhausted, I cut off the connection with my snare and let it dissipate into the air. I then collapsed to the floor, too tired to stand.

Immediately Rhys was by my side, his beautiful eyes anxious and concerned.

He reached out and grabbed my hand. "Are you all right?"

A tired half-laugh escaped my lips. "You're asking if I'm all right? I'm just tired. You're the one Osadyn tried to shish kebob."

"They were just physical wounds, practically healed already." He flashed me a smile, and once again I was struck by how much I loved this man. "It's one of the definite upsides of a Berserker's power."

"How did you 'zerk, at the end?" I asked.

Rhys gave me a rueful smile. "There's nothing like the thought of the one you love dying to get the adrenalin flowing. When I saw it bite you and pull you away from me... I snapped, and it couldn't stop my emotions." He helped me into a sitting position. "Don't worry about me, I'm more worried about what it took out of you to cast that snare and to... to bind Osadyn."

His last words held a question in them. How was it possible for me to bind Osadyn? I wasn't his Binder – Mallika was.

For a moment neither of us spoke, the bitter realization of what my binding Osadyn likely meant sinking into both of us, sucking out any feeling of triumph.

Mallika was dead.

CHAPTER 13

A MESSAGE FROM THE DEAD

T he door to the Berserker house was locked. Rhys didn't bother with the keys and simply ripped the door off its hinges. Aside from the door, the house appeared to be intact and there was no sign of any combat. That was a good sign.

Rhys and I had left the hotel ballroom before any emergency services had arrived. We had snuck out through a back entrance avoiding the throng of confused students huddled outside.

We hadn't spoken during the drive home, silently sharing the irrational fear that if we said anything about Mallika's possible death we might somehow make it real. We were trapped in a superstitious version of Schrödinger's cat – until we actually saw her dead there was still a chance that she might be alive.

A single light glowed from upstairs in an otherwise dark house. We walked in and turned on the downstairs lights, flooding the house with illumination.

"Hello?" Rhys called. "Mallika? Are you there?"

No answer.

I had a strange feeling of déjà-vu and was forcibly reminded of the night I awoke and knew Kara had died.

We ran up the stairs to Mallika's bedroom. The door was ajar and light spilled into the hallway.

Rhys paused and knocked on the door. "Mallika?"

Still no answer.

He pushed the door open.

Mallika's room was Spartan with a twin bed in the corner, a small desk and a tiny ledge mounted to the wall that held a bronze statue of a woman with ten arms holding weapons and riding on a lion. In the middle of the floor lay a chair turned over and out of place.

And hanging over the chair, gently swaying, was the body of Mallika, a noose around her neck.

With a gasp I turned away, but not before I caught a glimpse of her vacant, lifeless eyes staring out at me.

"No. No, no, no, no, no," said Rhys. He stared at Mallika his expression crumpling into a look of pure distress. "Why would you do this?"

I reached out and pulled Rhys into my arms. For several moments we stood there, locked in an embrace, seeking comfort and solace.

When Rhys finally pulled back, he said, "Why don't you go downstairs? I'll take care of things up here." He looked up at Mallika's swaying body. "I don't want to leave her like this."

Part of me really wanted to take him up on the offer and let him take care of everything. But I also knew that as hard as this had been for me to see, it had to be ten times worse for him. He had known her since she first became a Binder, which would have been fifty or sixty years ago.

"No, I'll help."

Rhys put the chair back upright and stood on it, gently lifting Mallika's body to give the rope some slack. I loosened the noose around her neck and pulled the rope off of her.

With extreme care, Rhys stepped down from the chair and placed Mallika's body onto her bed. He reached out a hand and closed her eyes. It was a simple gesture, but it left her looking much more peaceful and serene. I took a blanket from the closet and placed it over her.

We were about to leave when my eyes caught sight of something strange. In the center of Mallika's desk rested a sealed envelope with my name written on it in large loopy writing.

"Did you see this?" I asked, pointing at the envelope.

Rhys shook his head. "No. What is it?"

I picked up the envelope and turned it over in my hands. "I'm not sure. Some sort of letter addressed to me."

By wordless agreement, we went downstairs to read the letter, leaving Mallika in peace on her bed.

We sat at the kitchen table. I slid a finger beneath the sealed flap and pulled out several sheets of stationary. They read:

Dearest Madison,

I hope you will never read this letter, and I may tell you this information in person when you are ready to hear it. However, my intuition advises me to write down what I have learned. Just in case.

I have long known that you were no ordinary Berserker or Binder. How could you be? You had powers that no one had seen before and strange visions that none could explain.

But I did not know, and had little reason to suspect, just how unusual you are. It finally became clear to me when Sunee and Nakai came to test you with the Sarolt stone. From their reaction to your unique powers, I could tell they knew more than they were telling.

Even then, I might not have forced the issue if Sunee hadn't slipped by asking Nakai if you were "the one". At that time I promised you I would investigate, so I have been quietly meeting with other Berserkers and Binders asking discrete questions and learning what I could.

My efforts have paid off, and I have discovered a hidden piece of knowledge that seems to have been passed on to only a few in the Binder Conclave. I do not know whether it is a prophecy or simply information passed down from the lost origins of the Berserkers, but I do believe you have a right to know it.

The Binders have long believed that at some point in time, the magic keeping Verenix and the Havocs bound would start to corrupt. One of the effects of this corruption is that when a Berserker or Binder dies, his or her powers would be absorbed by a current Berserker or Binder, rather than a new initiate. The "one" Sunee referred to is this person to whom these powers are drawn. That person would have the ability to Bind – or free, if her life blood were spilled – multiple Havocs.

I believe you are that one. I believe that you have absorbed the powers of Eric and Kara and are now both Berserker and Binder for Pravicus and Margil.

The prophecy seems to hint that eventually all the Berserkers and Binders will die, save the one, leaving you with their combined powers. Then, when all their power has consolidated in you, you will have the ability to not just bind the Havocs, but to remove them completely. Whether that means you will be able to kill them or to simply send them back where they came from, I do not know.

This is a heavy burden, especially for one so young as yourself. If the fates are kind you will have many years to grow up before I need to reveal this to you.

I fear we may not have that long.

Sincerely,

Mallika

Placed underneath the signature was a sticky note with handwriting on it similar to the letter, only not as neat and precise. It was obviously written in a hurry.

Through my bond with Rhys I felt his anguish and knew you were on the verge of death. By ending my life I gave you the power to live. Do not be sad, for this is a sacrifice freely given. I have lived a long and full life and am at peace with my God.

Farewell.

Rhys and I sat in silence trying to take in everything Mallika had written. It seemed so overwhelming, so... big, that I had difficulty wrapping my mind around it. Not only was I a Berserker and a Binder, but it seemed like I was destined to be the last one standing.

The sound of a car pulling up let us know that the other

Berserkers were back from investigating the temperature spike. Rhys and I went out to meet them.

Clearly the temperature spike had not just been a false alarm. Shing, Davu, Josiah, and Arthur climbed out of the Range Rover, defeat written in every movement they made. Their clothes were ragged, and their expressions were so grim you would think someone had died.

Then I realized Aata was missing.

Like the last tumbler of a lock clicking into place, Mallika's words in the letter suddenly made sense. If Mallika's suspicions were correct, then those images that flashed in my head were glimpses of other people's memories - some sort of side effect of the power transfer.

Which meant that Aata was dead, too.

That flood of images before Osadyn had attacked would have fit perfectly - Maori warriors, the beaches of New Zealand, and the small boy fighting would all be significant images to him. The German village and the soccer match must have been memories from his Binder, who would have died when he did.

It was no surprise, but it was another grief to add to my rapidly expanding list, when Shing opened the back of the Range Rover and pulled out a figure wrapped in a blanket. Judging by the size, it had to be Aata.

Arthur, Davu, and Josiah came into the house while Shing carried Aata's body in through the garage. While he found a place to store Aata's body, the others told us what had happened.

The Berserkers had been monitoring the local temperatures. At 7:30 Aata discovered an anomaly in Astoria, a small town out at the coast.

Once they arrived, the signs of Margil's presence were clear. They found him waiting for them in a large cemetery surrounded by hundreds of reanimated corpses. These bodies weren't like the slowly shuffling zombies you see in the movies. They certainly didn't have a Berserker's speed and strength, but they were as fast and agile as the Bringers Osadyn used.

The Berserkers battled their way through the reanimated corpses to get to Margil, but Margil had no intention of fighting them directly. Once they had defeated his minions, he began to retreat. The standard protocol should have been to track him for a few more hours until they could force him into a location that didn't have so many dead bodies for the Havoc to reanimate.

Aata had a different idea.

He rushed Margil and tried to take him on by himself. He almost managed to do it, but Margil was able to pierce him through the throat with one of his long claws. While Aata struggled to get free, Margil pierced him through the heart with another claw and killed him.

At this point in the story something inside me snapped, and I was filled with the overwhelming desire for solitude. There had been so much death and killing in the last few days that I couldn't listen any more. I needed air, or space, or anything but being here and talking about monsters and the dead.

I stood up. "I've got to go," I said.

Rhys immediately was on his feet. "I'll take you home," he said.

"Thanks."

***

When we got to my house, Rhys walked me up to the front door. It was three in the morning and from outside I could see there was a light on in the living room.

"Do you want me to come in?" Rhys asked.

"No. I think I'm ready for tonight to be over." I reached up and kissed him on the cheek. "Goodnight."

I slipped in the door and walked down the hall to the living room where I found my dad asleep on the couch, the television tuned to some random infomercial. Clearly he had made a futile but well-meaning attempt at waiting up for me.

Watching him sleep, I was torn between exasperation that he couldn't seem to stop treating me like a little girl, and a warm feeling of joy that he truly loved me. Given all the death and monsters I had been dealing with lately, this whole little girl thing didn't seem so bad.

I sat down on the couch and laid my head on Dad's shoulder. He stirred and opened his eyes.

He yawned and stretched, sitting up straighter. "Oh, you're home."

"Yeah, I'm home," I said, and then unexpectedly the tears came. As much as I wanted to think of myself as grown-up – independent, tough and unstoppable – there were times like this when all I wanted was my daddy.

And so I cried in his arms while he held me, and I told him everything that had happened: Osadyn attacking at Prom and using his powers to soothe our 'zerking, the images that came to me, and how Mallika had died and I bound Osadyn.

When I was finished, Dad had a far-away look in his eyes. "It should be me," he said. "I should be the one dealing with all of this, not my teenage daughter." He took a deep breath, and tears began to stream down his face. "I feel so useless."

"You're not useless," I said. "You're my dad. I need you now more than ever."

Dad pulled me in tight and together we cried. We cried for lost friends, for fear for our loved ones, and for the certainty we both felt that the worst was still to come.

***

The next day I slept in past noon. Mom of course wanted to hear all the details about Prom, and so I told her how wonderful it had been. I left out the part about Osadyn crashing the party.

That afternoon, I got into Mom's car, and I drove. I needed time to come to grips with everything that had happened. Until recently I had never known someone who died. Now I knew far too many.

I ended up near the school, and on a whim I drove into the school parking lot. I parked on the far side of the lot, just outside of the dead woods.

Strange how I used to fear those woods. I now knew I was more dangerous than anything that could possibly be in there.

I 'zerked and ran to the clearing where I had first been attacked. It was also the place where I had first seen Rhys. Despite the months that had passed, the evidence of my battle lingered – broken trees and large gouges torn out of the ground.

Dropping the 'zerk, I found a fallen tree trunk that was about the right height and sat down. It was a truly glorious day. Bright and sunny, with a light wind that blew in the fresh scent of pine.

I closed my eyes and let my mind wander. This place still had meaning to me. I fought my first battle here, not knowing what my enemies were and doubting whether I should be allowed near normal people. It had been a turning point. Up until then I had been scared and alone. Afterwards, I knew there were others like me.

My life had changed completely since then. Eric, Kara, Mallika, Aata and his binder, Christine, had all died. I now held their powers within me – six sets of powers inside a single person. No, seven. I had already been a Binder and Berserker when this all started.

What did this even mean? What was I supposed to do with their power? Was I just the sum of their powers, or was I supposed to be something more?

Things were changing in the Berserker world. Constants that had held for thousands of years were starting to shift and change. Deep inside me, I knew this was just the beginning of bigger changes.

And that scared me.

How was I supposed to know what to do? I hadn't even learned the ins and outs of this new world yet. It wasn't fair that I should have to deal with it falling apart around me.

I pulled out Mallika's letter and reread it. The power keeping Verenex and the Havocs bound was starting to corrupt. Was there more to it than simply the power coalescing into me? My intuition told me – quite loudly – that there was.

I felt someone 'zerk and judging by the distance and direction it was near the school parking lot.

It had to be Rhys.

Who else would come all the way out here to find me? I followed Rhys in my mind, feeling him come closer. Maybe it was my imagination, but it almost seemed like I could tell it was Rhys by the feel of his 'zerk. Could the other Berserkers do that? I didn't know. It was one of a thousand things that I hadn't yet had time to learn.

Rhys stopped 'zerking before he entered the clearing.

"Mind if I join you?" he asked.

I shifted to make room for him on the log. He sat down next to me, and I rested my head on his shoulder.

"How are you?" he asked.

"Scared. Confused. Sad. Angry. Mix in several helpings of joy and gratitude and it makes for a confusing recipe."

Rhys took a deep breath. "Changes are coming," he said. "You feel it too?"

I nodded. "I haven't even learned how things are supposed to be, and now they're changing on me. How do I deal with that?"

Rhys bent his head down and kissed me. "The same way you have dealt with everything up until now – with grace and poise."

I smiled and snuggled into Rhys, enjoying the feel of his arms around me, the solidity of his chest, and the scent that surrounded him.

At that moment, I felt as if I were inside a bubble of calm. Chaos, death, and danger surrounded me, beating on the outside, trying to get in, but right here, right now, I was happy.

To be continued
in
Bonds That Break (The Havoc Chronicles Book 3)

ACKNOWLEDGEMENTS

First and foremost, I want to thank YOU. Yes, you reading this. I want to thank all of you who read Threads That Bind and enjoyed it enough to come back to the Berserker's world and see how the story continued in Unbound. Seeing your excitement and reading your reactions has been more than worth the effort to write the books. I am truly delighted that you have let me share this story with you.

Next, I want to thank all those people who helped make this book what it is:

Thanks to Sabine Berlin who was my alpha reader and biggest cheerleader throughout the writing of this book.

Thanks to editor extraordinaire, Nancy Fulda, for once again removing thousands of words and inserting hundreds of better ones in their place.

Thanks to Janyse Frerichs, Terri Barton, and Aaron Williams for using their keenly-honed minds to weed out typos and other errors and make Unbound as clean as possible.

Thanks to Tian Mulholland for using his many graphical talents to once again create an extraordinary cover. I am still in awe of his skill.

Thanks to my father, Tom Williams for building www.havocchronicles.com when I was too busy with life to make it happen. It has helped me connect with my readers in a way I couldn't before.

And finally, thanks to my wonderful children for letting their father read his books to them, even when they are old enough to read them on their own. Your cries of "Just one more chapter!" are music to my ears.

ABOUT THE AUTHOR

BRANT WILLIAMS never outgrew YA literature and thinks almost any book can be improved by the addition of magic, superpowers, or monsters. He graduated from Brigham Young University with a Bachelors degree in Psychology and a Masters Degree in Organizational Behavior. He lives near Portland, OR with his wife and four beautiful children who make him smile. This is not the first book he has written, but it is the first one he has made public.

You can find out more about Brant Williams and his books at www.havocchronicles.com or follow him on Twitter @wobblyg, or like Threads That Bind on facebook.com/Havocchronicles.

CPSIA information can be obtained at www.ICGtesting.com
Printed in the USA
LVOW101444140613

338656LV00015B/677/P